Foreword.

The miners' strike of 1984 was one of the r
controversial industrial events in the histor
union movement. Although the strike took
was three years earlier that industrial action
protest at the government's decision to clos
country, but the strike was halted when the government decided to scrap the plans. It was widely speculated that this was only a short temporary reprieve for the miners and the Yorkshire N.U.M. passed a resolution that strike action should take place if any mine was closed for reasons other than natural exhaustion or for reasons of geological difficulties.

In 1982 the miners accepted an offer of a 5.2 per cent pay rise despite the union's call for the offer to be rejected. Many people thought that by rejecting their leaders' calls for industrial action and accepting this offer that the miners were playing into the government's hands and that the government might see this as a sign of weakness in the union. In 1983 Ian McGregor (later to become Sir Ian McGregor) was put in charge of the National Coal Board, a man who had previously been put in charge of the British Steel Corporation and it was rumoured that he had saved the steel industry in this country almost turning it into a profit making industry. However the cost of this success was at the expense of the steel workers when he halved the workforce in the time that he was there. His appointment as head of the Coal Board caused speculation that he was brought in as a hatchet man and that he was there to close pits. This led to many confrontations with the miners president Arthur Scargill.

In 1984 the government announced that the agreement that had been drawn up with the N.U.M. in 1974 would no longer be in force and that 20 coal mines would be closed throughout the country and upwards of twenty thousand jobs would be lost, causing communities to lose their main source of employment. The government announced that 5 pits would be closed within 5 weeks causing some miners to start unofficial strike action. On the 12th of March miners' leader Arthur Scargill called for the unofficial strikes to be made official and asked for all miners in all areas to withdraw their labour and to make the strike official. The decision by the Colliery Officials Union (N.A.C.O.D.S.) not to strike caused tension among the striking miners but they put up the argument that if safety work was not done in the mine then the mines could rapidly deteriorate and be unsafe to return to causing them to be closed defeating the object of the strike.

South Wales miners were generally bitter that although they had appealed in the past for support when pits in Wales were being closed they were generally ignored, but now that the Yorkshire area was being threatened with closures and job losses everybody was expected to follow Yorkshire and down tools and come out on strike.But given the amount of pits in such a small area as Wales, the miners decided that they too were under threat and to support the strike seemed the logical thing to do. The strike originated in Yorkshire, with Scotland, Kent and the north east of England following rapidly behind with the Lancashire miners' leaders calling for strike action later in the month much against the wishes of their members who were still working. Pits in north Wales and the midlands were generally unresponsive to the strike while in Nottingham the Nottingham branch of the N.U.M. disagreed with the strike calling it unofficial until they were allowed to have a ballot of all the members. When a ballot was refused they continued to work causing most of the other areas to brand them as strike breakers or as some would put it more bluntly scabs, but they stood firm and continued to work, this ultimately led to Nottingham breaking away from the main body of the union to form the Union of Democratic Mineworkers (the U.D.M.).

The strike although basically not about money, but for job security soon turned into a political battle with neither the N.U.M. nor the government wanting to back down, but it later emerged that in the time between 1981 when the government had to back down to the miners and 1982 when miners accepted the 5.2 pay rise against the advice of their leaders that the conservative government had used the time to convert some power stations to use other fuel as well as coal to guard against the fate that caused their downfall in the 1972 and 1974 strikes.

They also used the time to stockpile coal and recruit haulage companies to continue to transport coal to the power stations and cross picket lines in the eventuality that the rail workers would support the miners and refuse to carry coal to the power stations.This ploy also allowed the electricity companies to avoid having to impose power cuts, another thing that had led to the miners being victorious in previous disputes, turning Maggie Thatcher from a one time milk snatcher to a job hijacker as one union official would later put it.

The strike lasted until 3rd of March 1985, with only the Kent miners voting to carry on with the strike. Some miners had already returned to work before the strike was officially over although the government later admitted that the numbers that they had used were hugely exaggerated to destroy the miners' morale. The unions were also running short of funds which were being used to fund picketing and many miners were starting to feel the effects of the winter as the scraps of coal that they would scavenge from slag heaps had also dwindled out causing many to resort to cutting trees down to keep their homes warm which caused some to be arrested and charged with trespassing and theft. Also in some areas working miners were being attacked and their families being threatened and abused, and in south Wales there was the tragic death of a taxi driver who was killed when a concrete block was dropped through the window of his car while he was taking a miner to work. But even through all this, it was only by a very narrow margin that the vote to return to work was won.

On March the 5th 1985 the miners returned to work with their heads held high not bowed in defeat as the government would like to think. Some were led back to work by brass bands while others returned silently as if they had never been away, but whatever way they returned they all had one thing in common: their pride was still intact and the ones who had lasted the whole strike knew that whatever the Tory government did to them to break their spirit failed. In some cases it was good to be back as now they could feed their families and not have to rely on handouts from some people that they did not know, and also the people in the towns and villages that had supported them in this long and sometimes bitter dispute could now be thanked, for if it was not for the kindness and generosity of these people the miners would have been starved back to work long ago by this calculating and uncaring government whose only aim was to bring down the miners regardless of the cost to the country and in some respects to life itself.
The strike had collapsed into chaos with the some of the union leaders seemingly at loggerheads,arguing that the strike should carry on. It seemed to be turning into a personal crusade for Arthur Scargill to wage his own war on the conservative government and to fuel his own ambitions to move onto the political bandwagon.

Many people involved in the strike were quick to point out that if Scargill had given the Nottingham miners a vote as they were entitled to then the strike may not have occurred or possibly would only have lasted a short time as in 1972 and 1974, but in his own egotistical way he remained adamant that he held a mandate to call strike action from an earlier vote.

This is a story of a group of friends and miners who stayed out on strike for the full duration, and some of their escapades at home and as they travelled around the country on various picketing duties.

The silent wheels (big boy's story) Chapter 1

4th MARCH 1984 4.30 AM

It was a typically cold march morning in South Wales as big Jones rose from his bed at 4.30 a.m. to do his usual shift at the local colliery. Big Jones as he was known by everybody who had the good fortune to have known him was a great big man with hands the size of a bag of coal -- and a heart just as big. He was so big, as his good friend Alfie used to say, if he asked him to wash his back in the showers at the end of their shift in the mine,

"I would rather wash a Tesco's window than wash your back."

He had to leave for the 5.00 a.m. bus; he had a feeling in his ample stomach that something was about to happen, something that could change the rest of his life. Before he left he had his usual breakfast of a large helping of fruit and a glass of cold water that he put in the fridge to chill the night before, something that he had done every night for as long as he could remember, and this would be rounded off with a very loud burp to wash it down.

As he shouted so long to his wife he stepped out into the cold Welsh morning, locking the door and venturing out on to the frosty footpath, and over the frost covered grass to the house of his workmate Dillwyn, a man known as DD, (Dull Dill) to all who had the pleasure of knowing him, calling out over the fence "come on boy, the bus will be here in a minute."

Dillwyn came out of his door wearing his usual thick coat, and as grumpy as normal, groaning to big Jones.

"What are you so happy about?"

"Come on," said the big fella, "we'll be late."

"Who cares" said DD in his normal early morning grumpy way.

As the bus came around the corner, the boys could see that there was someone on the bus who was not normally up at this time of day. King Will (as he was known) the pit secretary of the union was occupying the front seat; the boys could just make out the outline of his ample nose against the darkness of the bus. Some would say that before Will was born God had asked him what type of nose he would like to have. Will was a little short of hearing and he thought God said what type of rose would you like, and he replied: "Give me a big red one." God duly obliged and Will has one of the finest nostrils in the valleys, peppered with a few blackheads the size of blackcurrants for good measure.

"What are you doing here" said Big Jones with a wicked grin and

flashing a set of teeth a Hollywood star would pay good money for.
"He must be sleep walking," said DD "Will have never been up this early since his house was flooded."
" Don't start," said King Will, "the news is not good."
"Must be something up," said Big Jones, "it would take an earthquake to get Will out of bed this early in the morning."
As the bus pulled up outside the pithead baths, the boys could see all the lodge committee were sitting in the canteen drinking tea and looking much fed up.
"Must be serious" said Big Jones, "the last time we saw all these together in the morning, was when they heard that there was free beer checks in the Gordon's club, and they wanted to be first in the queue".
"Too right," said Oddball, the first aid man, "I might have to give them the kiss of life",
"You're all right," said Big Jones "I would rather have all my teeth out than kiss that lot, they are as ugly as a £50 fine"

Dai Rugby was there, he was so short that he was the only treasurer in the South Wales coal fields who used to take a high chair to meetings. Then there was Jamie, the vice chairman, he had been married so many times, that he had to go to the Betty Ford clinic in America to cure his addiction to wedding cake and sherry. Sitting on the right hand side of King Will was his sidekick, and lodge chairman, Ivor (the mountain man) John. Ivor was born in a little village in the back of beyond. The village was so high up in the mountains, that they say that God was his neighbour; indeed they still do not get milk in bottles. The rest of the lodge were Peter (the poser) Evans, an electrician by trade. He had a mop of black curly hair which some say was due to the fact that he once put a screwdriver into a live generator on the top of the pit to see if it was still working. As he was soon to find out it was working as Peter disappeared into a cloud of smoke, and the pit and everything within 10 miles of the pit was plunged into darkness for many hours, causing untold chaos.

The last one of the lodge was Norman the Dwarf, he was half an inch taller than Dai Rugby, but not so wide. It is rumoured that while Norman was in the army he was on sentry duty, one dark night in some far away jungle where he heard a noise in the undergrowth. "Who goes there" said the dwarf in his most menacing voice. After issuing the warning two more times, he heard a strange sound coming back at him, which he took as a strange language, possibly an enemy, so he opened fire as a good sentry would. Hearing a loud crashing sound, which he took to be his enemy falling to his death; he stealthily crept forward with his gun still cocked and ready to go again when he came to a sudden stop. There on the floor in front of him riddled with army issue bullets, was a donkey, stone dead with all four legs up in the air. The dwarf had two choices when the farmer who owned the donkey complained to his senior officers, either strap the plough to his back and work the farmer's land as the donkey had done, or pay for a new donkey. Some say he must have done a deal with the farmer, because he had a set of false teeth which must have been taken from the donkey. Altogether these lodge members were known as the simple six.

All together they were a formidable outfit,with faces which only a mother could love. These boys feared nobody. King Will rose to his feet, wiping the last traces of the sleep that was stuck in the corner of his eyes.
" Boys" he said "this is sad day for us all."
"It must be," said Stumpy sitting in front of King Will, "anything that can get you out of bed before dinner time must be serious."

Stumpy was one of the older members of the union, in fact it is rumoured, that when they sank the pit, he was sitting at pit bottom with a dinosaur on a piece of rope.
"This is serious," said Will. "Our comrades up in Yorkshire have gone on strike and are asking for an all-out strike."
"Hold on Will," came a booming voice from the back of the canteen that everybody recognised as Howler the face captain. Now Howler was a man who had a lot of influence with the boys who worked in his team and it was common knowledge that he once sang with Tom Jones in his local rugby club and some say that Howler was the better singer, the only thing that let him down was that he looked like a monkey.
"Last month we were up in Yorkshire asking for support when they shut a pit down in the Rhondda and we were told to go home as it was our fight and nothing to do with them. So why all of a sudden is it our fight now, I'll tell you why because they are shutting pits up there now and they are starting to panic, that's why." This met with a healthy round of applause from all the boys in the canteen, especially the boys who had been in Yorkshire with Howler.
"Come on now boys," said King Will, "we all know that this government wants to shut all the pits, especially in South Wales, and the only way to fight them is to stand together".
"Come on now boys," said Dai rugby, to shouts of "Stand up Dai, we can't see you."
"I was up in Yorkshire and it was not very nice how we were treated, and what they said to us, but Will is right we have got to stand together if we want to fight for our jobs."
"Boys we could stand here arguing all day," said Will, "but the thing

is what happened up in Yorkshire is in the past, we have now got to look to the future and unite if we want to save our jobs."

This was met with a mixture of comments some of which cannot be put into words here. Most of the boys had been here before (72&74), (indeed some say that Stumpy was in the great strike) and were sceptical about the outcome of another strike. In fact many thought that if they wanted to shut the pits they would do so anyway, and maybe a strike may make them close the pits sooner.

The meeting went on until around 9-00 a.m. and it was decided that we would all go home , and accept the lodge recommendation for industrial action, with a meeting to be held in the community centre on the following Friday for a further vote and an update of the situation. As the boys got on the buses to go home there were differences of opinion, and some wondered what they were going to do in the next week.

"Well I'll be going up the mountain with my dog," said Big Jones, "if I stay in the house with my wife I think she will make me do more than I do in work."

"That's not hard," said DD, "you don't do a lot any way."

"What you mean", said the big boy, "I look after you like a mother."

"I'll be going up the club out of the way," said Stumpy, "the missus would kill me if we were in the house together all day."

"Nice to have plenty of money" said Colin Asthma taking a puff of his inhaler,

"What are you on about?" came the reply. "You're on the committee so you won't be short of money; you haven't paid for a pint since Winston Churchill was a boy."

The week went by pretty slowly with the boys passing the time doing various things: Stumpy did spend a lot of time in the club,Big Jones did go walking with his dog, and Colin Asthma did make himself available for more committee duties, which he did get, much to a lot of comments from the boys, which were like water off a duck's back. Colin was a keen fisherman and one afternoon he and Stumpy went for a walk down to the local park where there was a fishing competition going on. As they sat on a bench watching, Colin noticed a young boy having a problem casting his reel into the water and noticed that he had not caught any fish.Colin went over and knelt down by the boy and whispered in his year that he knew where he was going wrong and asked the boy to give him his rod and he would show him. The boy gave Colin his rod and Colin cast out into the lake, as soon as he cast out he could feel the line going tight and he turned to the boy with a look of great pleasure on his face and he said to him, "You see son all you need is a bit of know how."

But the boy was just looking out into the lake, as were a lot of the other fishermen, and as Colin looked up he could see what they were all looking at. Colin had cast his line out and a duck gone for the bait on the line and got tangled up in the line and Colin was reeling a duck in instead of a fish. As he looked around he could see Stumpy almost crying with laughter, so Colin gave the rod back to the boy with the duck still making all sort of noises and furiously trying to get free and told the boy,
"Well there you are I've shown you how to cast a line into the water, so best of luck."
and with those few kind words Colin got out of there as fast as he could leaving the boy with a duck on his line and Stumpy not being able to move off the bench, where he was in tears of laughter.

Friday soon came and the community centre was full, with a lot of complaints because the bar was closed and would not be opened until after the meeting was over, a wise decision because a lot of these boys did not need alcohol to get them going. Alfie sat between Lou and Stumpy, a bad choice of seats as he was soon to find out. He forget that Lou was deaf in his right ear, and Stumpy was deaf in his left ear. Alfie sat on Lou's right and Stumpy's left side, so when the meeting started and all the seats were taken he was stuck there.

As the meeting started Alfie began to regret his choice of seats. Lou was first to talk nudging, him sharply in the ribs asking
"What did he say then", and before he could answer Stumpy would stick his elbow in his other side.
"What's he on about? I can't hear a thing; tell him to speak up."
"Why didn't you two sit closer" said Alfie rubbing his sore ribs, "it's like sitting between a pair of monkeys, but then a monkey has a brain different to you two." This comment brought more rib ticklers making him sorry that he had said anything in the first place.

By the end of the meeting Alfie felt he had been trampled on by the Welsh rugby team, and he did not know much about the meeting, as he was more concerned about dodging the flying elbows of his two mates, and trying to repeat to them what he did hear. As they left the meeting Big Jones came up with a solution to all their problems.
"Let's go for a pint", said the big fella. This suggestion did not get many arguments except who was buying the first round. Stumpy thought Colin Asthma should pay.
"You're on the committee and you won the tote last night."
"In shares with the wife and her sister," said Colin. "I didn't get

anything out of it".
"You always say that every time you win something," came the retort from DD, causing all the boys to nod their heads in agreement.
Once in the local club after much arguing and debating who should buy the first round Stumpy reluctantly went to the bar, and Ivor the bar as he was known, the club steward, came out with a plate of sandwiches for free.
"If you want I'll draw you a map," said Big Jones, "as you don't go to the bar that often."

Stumpy came back with five pints, mumbling that he'd been caught and that he would make sure that they would all buy a round before they went home . Colin Asthma sat down on his return from the toilet to Stumpy's taunts of "better do something about the prices in the club for the boys on strike."
"What can I do? I don't own the place."
"Well you're on the committee, volunteer to do some extra duties for nothing and donate the money to the boys on strike."
"Nelson would have more chance of getting his eye back" commented Alfie. The afternoon passed and Stumpy did manage to get all the boys to buy a round of drinks, they even managed to get Stumpy to go to the bar a second time, which was very rare, and Big Jones even managed to devour some more sandwiches which one of the locals brought in for the boys to go with the ones they had already eaten.

As they left the club Big Jones and DD decided to take a short cut home across the fields, which turned out to be a bad idea as the ground was soggy due to the heavy rain of the previous night, and they were constantly up to their ankles in mud. At one point DD lost his shoe and had to go on his hands and knees to get them out of the swamp-like mud. This caused much amusement to Big Jones, but the smile was soon to be wiped off his face

.

"Come on boy," said the big fella. "I can feel the beer and sandwiches starting to work."
"Too bad," said his mate, "that's what you get for drinking all the beer that was left and eating so much food." DD was purposely walking slowly, as he knew, from experience that when the big fella had been on the beer, and needed to use a toilet he could not wait long. As he went as fast as he could go DD tried to hold him up as much as possible breaking into constant fits of laughter. At last his house was in sight, and he rushed up the path with his buttocks firmly clenched reaching into his pocket for his front door key but when he put his hand into his pocket for his key, he found to his horror that he

did not have a key -- he must have left it at home in the morning. Frantically he began knocking at the door, and calling out to his wife as he stood there in sheer terror at the thought of what was about to happen in his underpants if the door was not opened in the next few seconds. At last his wife came to the door,

"Out of the way," he yelled rushing past her like an Olympic 100 metre runner.

"Hang on," said his wife.

"Can't stop," he said as he ran up the stairs with his trousers already at half mast. "This is an emergency," he shouted as he pushed the toilet door open, and threw his ample backside on to the toilet. Suddenly he felt a great sense of relief as his bowels emptied with a thunder that must have been heard for miles, but, along with this came a feeling of warm wetness up his back, and he could smell fresh paint which he could not remember smelling in the morning. Forcing himself to look down he could see that where the hole in the toilet should be was covered by a board that his wife must have been standing on to paint the toilet ceiling. Rising to his feet Big Jones could see that not only had he made the board unusable but he had also pebble dashed the toilet wall, and the contents of his bowel had shot up as far as the top of his back and into his hair.

After a lengthy time in the toilet the red faced big fella emerged to see his wife standing there, with the paint brush still in her hand and an expression on her face that he knew too well meant that it would be better to say nothing.

"I was trying to tell you I was painting the toilet ceiling, and I had put a board across the toilet to stand on," she said "but you flew past me so fast I could smell your shoes burning: good enough for you anyway," she said, "and if you think that I'm going to paint the ceiling again, think again, because you are going to do it." As he sank himself into the bath he thought to himself: I hope the boys don't find out about this, but there was more to come.

The following morning big Jones awoke at his usual time long before the sun came up, and to his surprise his wife, who was still not very happy with him was not far behind him.

"How are you up early?" he said. "You don't start work until 8 o'clock; go back to bed and I'll make you a cup of tea and some toast."

"You can stuff the tea and toast, and don't try to butter me up either. I want that toilet wall and ceiling painted by the time I get home from work."

"But," he replied, "You know the smell of paint makes me sick."

"Yes," said his wife, "and what you left yesterday made me sick, so just do as I tell you, or do you want me to tell all the boys?" The big fella did not have much option but to do as he was told and reluctantly he went to the shed to get a paint brush and paint.

When his wife got home from work she was amazed to find the toilet was freshly painted.
"I never thought you would finish it today" she said with a sarcastic tone to her voice.
"What do you mean? I can paint when I want to,"came the answer in an equally sarcastic tone. Little did she know that as soon as she went to work he asked his next door neighbour if he knew anybody who was handy with a paintbrush, to which his neighbour replied that his son in law was out of work and would do it for some beer money.
"Phone him," he replied. "I'll give him ten pounds if he does it today, but not a word to anyone, especially my missus."
"Anyway get dressed we're going out."
"Where we going to go?" she said. "I'm not going to the club. All you will do there is talk about what you lot are going to do if the strike lasts longer than you think, and then Stumpy will start singing when he has a drink."
"Well," said Big Jones, "you always say you like Stumpy's singing."
"Yes," she said, "but it would be nice if he knew more than two songs."
"Come on then, get dressed and we'll go down to town."

Chapter 2

As they waited for the bus to town Big Jones was hoping that nobody had found out about him paying for the paintwork to his toilet, but trouble lay ahead in a different form. As they boarded the bus he heard a familiar voice booming from the back seat.
"Where you going comrade?" Big Jones knew immediately without looking up that it was Lou.
"As far away from you as possible," he said laughing as he said it.
"Come up here my darling," he said to Big Jones's wife, "I always said you were too good for him." As the bus carried on into town the two friends continued to wind each other up until the bus started to pull into the main terminal. Sitting about half way up the bus there was a boy of about 20 years old who suddenly put his leg out as a man of about 60 was trying to pass with his wife.
"Nobody gets off this bus until I say," he said.
Big Jones said to Lou, "We'll see about that!"
"Leave it there," said his wife "I told you this morning that I want no nonsense out of you after what you did yesterday."

"What did he do?" said Lou,"
"Never mind," said Jones as he started to walk down to the front of the bus.
"I said no bo…" That was as far as he got as a fist the size of a frozen turkey slammed into his jaw sending his chin one way and his teeth another way as he went down quicker than a punctured tyre.
"Quick," said Lou, " let's get off the bus before he calls the police."
"He won't wake up for some time," said the man who had been trying to pass him,with a welcome smile on his face. The rest of the night passed off with no more excitement, apart from Lou trying to find out what Jones had done the previous day, and his wife refusing to talk to him whenever the subject of the day before was mentioned, but Lou made a promise that he would find out and when he did he would make the big fella beg him not to tell anybody, but it might be too good to miss.

The following day Lou couldn't wait to get to the club before Big Jones to tell everybody what had happened on the bus, and to find out if anybody knew his secret. As Big Jones walked into the club it was obvious that Lou had told them all when as soon as he walked into the bar everybody started to sing the Rocky theme tune.
"Had a pint or two last night I heard," said Stumpy with a big grin on his face, "the trouble with you boy is, after a few drinks you think you're Two-can Van Damme".

The following week all the boys met at the canteen at the pit. King Will was there at his desk, once again the centre of attention and surrounded by the rest of the lodge committee.
"Right," said Will. "Who will be doing picket duties?"
There was a lot of grumbling and at last Stumpy said, "Will it be like the other strikes, when all your cronies had the best places and all we had was what nobody else wanted?"
"You know I don't do things like that," said Will, "I always try to be fair."
"Where do you want us to go then?" asked Colin Asthma, before taking a puff on his inhaler.
"First of all boys, we must get organised. Who has got cars they will use, and we can sort out paying petrol expenses."
"How far do you think we will be going then?" asked Lou. "Last time we were outside local private mines and delivery yards. Will it be the same or are we going to go further or will we be in the area?"
"We will have to have a meeting of the lodge and come back to you as soon as we can."

King Will and his lodge members, or Will and the simple six as they

were known to the boys, hurriedly went into the lodge and emerged after about half an hour.
"What we intend to do boys is we must go to all the local coal yards and ask them for their support. If they refuse we will put picket lines there. There is also an opencast coal site and we'll do the same there. But make sure the coal traders are told we will let them deliver to schools and hospitals and anywhere else that are priorities, like old people's homes and pensioners."
"Does that mean that Stumpy will get his coal then?" said Big Jones.
"He should. It has been said that he is the oldest man in the world."
"Too right," said Colin, "he still owes Jesus a fiver."
All these comments brought a lot of laughter and a few grumblings from Stumpy, but all in all it was taken in good humour.

When things were decided, and the boys agreed what they would be doing, and who would be going with whom and where they were going to go, they got together and decided what time they would meet and whose cars they would be using. Stumpy, Lou, Big Jones and Alfie were together and they would use Lou's car first. DD, Colin Asthma, Leighton and Morgan decided they would go together and Colin would use his car.

The first week was spent going around the coal yards and various places in the town and asking them for support and explaining that they were in dispute with the coal board about closing pits and not about money. Most of the time the words just fell on deaf ears.
As the weeks went by the boys started to feel the effects of not having money in their pockets and boredom set in if there was not something to do. Some of the boys had allotments to escape to if they were bored or if their wives were nagging them, others like Colin would go fishing, or like Big Jones would take his dog up the mountain in the morning and not come back until the middle of the day. Stumpy as usual would escape to the club.

Every Saturday morning the boys who had been on picket would meet in the community centre to claim the money they would be allowed for doing picket duties. The money was £2.50 per day not a lot but it was better than nothing, and at least it was getting them out of the house for a couple of hours. The car drivers would get £3.00 per day and 15p per mile for the petrol. Dai Rugby the treasurer would pay the money out but what the boys would do was get their money and then go back up and say they forgot to ask for their petrol money. It all worked out fine for a while until he caught on after he realised that the dwarf was asking for petrol money and he was in Dai's car, and everybody knew that the dwarf was too short to see out of the windscreen without a booster seat.

There is a story about the dwarf, that he started to have driving lessons and everyone was surprised that he actually got up to test standard. On the day of his test he successfully completed the course, with the exception of nearly killing a traffic warden who was trying to cross the road on a pedestrian crossing, and taking a corner too fast and almost going up the town hall steps. But when he was asked questions on the highway code he came up with one of his finest answers, even by his standards. He was asked, "What signs would you expect to see on a country road?" To which he replied, "Farm fresh eggs 25p a dozen, and bed and breakfast £5.00 a night." It is rumoured that the examiner was last seen in the centre of the town with a vacant look on his face and asking people the way to the nearest chemist so that he could get some tablets; needless to say he never worked again.

The boys were all given places to visit and ask for support and split up into their groups. Big Jones, Stumpy, Lou and Alfie were together and they would use Lou's car, and Big Jones would be the spokesman, as he was the biggest, and slightly the more intelligent. The first place they went to was a local coal yard they thought was selling to people other than pensioners which was the agreement. The coal yard was on a local trading estate opposite a number of factories, and this was where Big Jones once again was caught with his trousers down so to speak.

It was on a Tuesday morning, and Jones had a strange feeling in his ample stomach and had to find a toilet as quickly as possible, or he would be in trouble. Looking around he could see no toilets anywhere and he did not have time to try find a factory toilet so he made a dash for some waste land and got down behind a rock where he found great relief until he stood up with his trousers still around his ankles he heard a loud cheering and clapping, and upon looking upwards towards the factories opposite he saw a gang of women hanging out of the windows and cheering for the show they had just witnessed.

Chapter 3

As the strike drew on the boys were sent to more places to try to get support, or if they had money they would go to the club where the stories of their travels would be told over a few beers. One story was of Big Jones and his gang and a trip to Coventry, where it was reported a local private mine was still working. King Will had heard of this mine and sent the boys there to picket the place and ask them for support. The four boys decided toe keep the money they were given for a bed and breakfast, and as it was in the summer and they would be there for three days they decided to take a tent and use the money for other expenses. On arriving at the place that they were directed to they found it was very isolated and as it was late they pitched the tent and started a fire with some wood they gathered and opened the food parcels they had been given before they went on their travels, and the cans of beer they had bought before they left.

After a while they decided to get some sleep so they would be fresh in the morning.
The morning came with the boys all feeling stiff and tired after a night listening to Stumpy snoring, and blaming each over for the noises and smell in the tent. After a pitiful attempt to make some tea on the fire to go with the sandwiches they had kept over from the night before, the boys decided to look for the entrance to the mine and then go and see if they could find a café or somewhere where they could get some food. On locating the gates to the private mine it seemed very quiet, so they decided to send Alfie and Lou to find somewhere to get some food.

As Alfie and Lou set off Stumpy and Big Jones settled down in the fold away chairs they had brought with them to wait for somebody to come to the mine. As Big Jones was watching for any sign of life at the mine he heard the sound of snoring and as he turned to look at Stumpy he could see that he was fast asleep,
"Hey wake up boy!" he shouted as he playfully pushed his slumbering mate.
"What's the matter with you?" asked a startled Stumpy.
"You were fast asleep boy," answered the big fella, "you were snoring like a horse boy."
"I was only resting my eyes," he retorted "and I don't snore."
"Well you had your eyes shut so you must have been sleeping," said Big Jones.
Quick as a flash Stumpy retorted,
"I had my boots on too but I wasn't walking, was I?"
Big Jones just laughed and he said, "Alfie is right about you,he told me that you had tight skin."
"What does he mean tight skin? He's losing his mind," Stumpy grunted.
"Well he reckons that every time you sit down your eyes close," replied big Jones.
Stumpy just looked at the big boy but did not say a word, he knew when he was beat.

"Where's the silver fox?" said Lou referring to Stumpy's silver hair as he calls it (everybody else calls it grey) on his return.
"Gone for a walk" said Big Jones.
"Anything happening at the mine?" asked the boys.
"All quiet" replied Big Jones, and he went on to tell them about how Stumpy fell asleep and the remark about his tight skin.
Stumpy returned after a little while and the boys were getting stuck into the rolls and coffee that Lou and Alfie had brought back.
"Hope you kept some for me," he said.
"Yes," said Lou, "We've kept you a crust."
"Very funny," he said tearing open the packet that was thrown at him, as he tried to eat and have a go at Alfie at the same time. The rest of the day was spent patiently waiting for somebody to turn up for work, and as night fell the boys decided to return to the tent which was only a short walk from where they were waiting.

Again the hours were passed away with a little bit of chit chat amongst themselves, and although it was near nightfall it was quite a nice evening. Eventually the boys decided to call it a night and if it was still quiet in the morning they would wait until the afternoon and phone back home to the lodge and say how quiet it was. Morning came after another restless night and Lou decided to go for an early morning walk. On returning from his walk he told the boys that he had found a country pub about a mile from where they were, and they all decided to wait until 12-00 o'clock and if there was no movement they would go and see if they could find some food.

The hours slowly passed and they were all in agreement that as soon as they got home they were going straight into the bath as they were all itching after spending two nights in a cramped up tent.
"I wish we went to a bed and breakfast" said Stumpy. "I was made for comfort not squashed up to Lou with big boy's feet stuck in my mouth all night."
"That was the only way to stop you snoring," said Jones,
"Yes," said Alfie, "it was worse than your singing, at least then we can all shout so we can't hear you."
"What you mean?" said Stumpy. "You didn't moan when I sang in the club last week and I gave you all a pint each out of the checks they gave me."
"They only gave you the checks to shut you up," said Lou, who brought laughter from the boys, and a grunt from Stumpy, but they all knew that he was right and he could give a nice song when he wanted to.

Twelve o'clock finally arrived and they all climbed into Lou's car to go to the pub that Lou had found. After a short drive they pulled up into the car park.

"Listen Jones," said Alfie. "Leave us order food first because once you start you eat two more spuds than a pig." "What do you mean?" said Jones. "I'm eating salad now."

"Salad," said Lou. "You'll eat the pattern off the plate if you get a chance."

On entering the pub the boys could see a big log fire and even though it was a nice day it felt really comfortable.

"Three pints and an orange juice please," said Jones.

"You must be bad boy," said Stumpy. "I've never known you to go to the bar first unless they were giving beer away, or somebody else was paying."

"You must be joking. I've bought you enough beer over the years, to sail a ship on," came the reply.

"The only ship he's been on is the ark," shouted Lou.

The boys all ordered homemade pie and eagerly wolfed it down.

"You could swear you boys haven't had a good meal for days," said the watching barman.

"We haven't," said Lou between mouthfuls of veg and pie.

"Where you boys from?" said the barman.

"Wales," said Stumpy rising from his chair to get more drinks.

"What are you doing here then? It's quiet here this time of year."

"We are on strike back home, working in the pits and they told us there was a private mine up here, which was still producing coal, and we came here to ask them to support us as it could be them that could be shut down next."

Stumpy returned to his seat with the drinks and started to finish his meal, when Big Jones asked the barman "Do you know this area at all?"

"Yes I was born here and have lived here all my life, why do you ask?"

"Well we have been picketing a mine just down the road, but it is quiet there, and we were wondering if they have gone on strike",

The barman asked Jones where exactly the mine was and when Jones explained he just asked,

"How long have you been there?"

"Two nights," replied the boys almost together,

"Well," he replied with a smile on his face, "the place you have just described has been closed for 3 years. The place you should have gone to is 10 miles further on up the road."

On returning from the trip to Coventry the boys tried to keep quiet about the little mishap but the story did get out and they did have a few remarks but all in all they took it well, but little did they know there was more to come before the strike came to an end?

Chapter 4

One Saturday after a meeting most of the boys collected their money for various picketing duties and they decided to go to the club opposite the pit to have a drink. Howler along with Stumpy after a few drinks were as usual leading the singing when they were interrupted by two travellers selling some rugs and carpets for what seemed like a giveaway price from a van parked outside the club. They brought out their merchandise into the club and rolled them out on to the floor for all to see, and asked for offers for the rugs.Howler saw a chance to get on his wife's good side, as he told the dwarf,
"I forgot to get my missus a birthday card and present so this might get me back in her good books."
"How much do you want?" he asked,
"£20 pound," said the man in a broad Irish accent.
"I'll give you ten," Howler replied.
The traveller looked at Howler and said, "Fifteen, and I'm making no money."
"Done," said Howler pulling the money out of his pocket and bending down to pick the rug off the floor.
"No, not that one," said the traveller,"that's the one we use for show, and it's dirty. I'll get you one from the van," he said.

As he put the money into his pocket his partner went out to the van and brought him a rug in a plastic bag, and the two men quickly walked out of the club, leaving Howler standing there with this rug in his hands and a big smile on his face.
"If I were you I would open that before they go," said Colin Asthma, "you can't trust these people."
Howler gave Colin a long look but all the same he took the rug out of the plastic bag, only to discover that all that he had bought was the rim of the rug with no centre to it. Running quickly to the door all he could see was the van disappearing around the bend in a cloud of smoke.
"Well I've heard of the hole in the wall gang," said the dwarf, "but these must been the hole in the rug gang."
"Where have you been hiding?" said Howler "under the table, because I didn't see you come in."
"I've been here ages," he replied.
"Well you must have been in disguise, because nobody's seen you,"

said Colin Asthma.
"I was the army hide and seek champion for years," he said. "I was once on a training exercise, where there was a voluntary camouflage exercise. A couple of us didn't bother to go, as it was early in the morning, and we were out on the beer the night before," he went on. "When the sergeant major told me the following day, in his usual sarcastic tone, when we were on parade that he didn't see me on the exercise, I just replied "Thank you very much sir," but he never saw the funny side and I ended up peeling potatoes in the army jail for a week."

Big Jones told the boys that they had won £50.00 on the tote the night before so they decided to go back to the local club to have a few beers. It was while they were there that they were given a tip on a horse which they decided to do. Their luck must have been in as they won £15.00 each, so they decided to stay a bit longer. It was the day that the local pigeon club were meeting after sending their birds on a race, and they sat down to have a pint and a chat. Alfie and Stumpy were talking to one of the pigeon boys by the bar and you could see him pointing to where Big Jones and the boys were sitting, when the pigeon owner walked over and sat down by Lou.
"I hear you keep pigeons" he said, and started to talk non stop about different breeds of birds, and the types of races they could be entered for.
Lou decided he had enough of this man and asked him, "Why are you telling me about pigeons?"
The man replied, "Because your mates told me that you keep pigeons," he said pointing at Alfie and Stumpy, who along with all the boys were now having a laugh at his expense,
but Lou had the last laugh as he told the man, "No, they have got it wrong. I've got chickens and those two are short sighted." In fact Lou did have a chicken, named Emile (which he pronounced a meal), which he kept in a pen in his garden.

As the strike started to turn from days to weeks, the boys were starting to get bored of doing nothing, even though they knew that in the long term it was still a fight for jobs, not money, and most of the local community knew this and mostly they supported them. A lot of people would give them any odd jobs to do, as Stumpy would constantly say to Colin Asthma
"You have never done so many duties in the club."
"What do you mean?" came the reply, "I'm always doing my duties."
"But you never used to call bingo before", said Stumpy, "you were always saying you could'nt sit up on the stage because you were scared of heights, and what about the time you had to stop the bingo

because you forgot your glasses. You said that you'll never do it again."
"It's better than being a bouncer in Mothercare," said Lou.
"That's where he buys all his clothes," said Big Jones.
"No need for that big boy, I'm only small because you used to eat my food when we were small."
"What do you mean when we were small, you're still small," said Big Jones.
"Yes," said Colin Asthma, "you're too short to go to a long dance," which brought howls of laughter from the other boys.

King Will had a phone call from the union head office in Cardiff saying that there would be a march in London, and the simple six decided that a bus would be provided to take some of the boys to take part. On the morning of the march it was a pleasant May morning and everybody going had to be outside the colliery by 4.00 a.m. to be in London by 9.00 a.m.
"What are we leaving so early for?" asked DD with one eye still closed.
"Because the police will be stopping the busses to try to stop us miners going up to London," said big Jones. "Won't take much to stop me," said DD, "I'm ready to go back to bed"
"Just pretend you're in work and we'll wake you when we get there," said Colin Asthma.This was met with a few muffled remarks as DD went back to sleep.

The journey to London was a long and tedious one, with some of the boy's playing cards, but most of them did do the same as DD and tried to go back to sleep, with the exception of King Will and the simple six who sat at the front of the bus planning what they would do on the march. As they suspected they were stopped by the police as they approached the Severn Bridge, but King Will produced a letter from the union head office which stated that they were all part of an official protest group and after a few phone calls they were left to go on their way.
"I don't trust them," said Big Jones. "I bet they will have the helicopters out watching us."
"Who do you think we are, the A team?" said Colin.
The rest of the journey was fairly uneventful apart from DD waking to find everybody looking at him and laughing.
"What are you lot laughing at?" he said in his grumpiest voice, but nobody answered.

As the bus neared London, King Will decided to ask the driver to make a toilet stop before they got into the city, and it was there that

DD found out what the laughter was on the bus. As he was getting of the bus in the services he could see people giving him funny looks, and pointing at him.
"What do they think they are looking at" he said to Big Jones,
"Don't know," came the reply, "perhaps they think you're a TV star."
"Aye," said Stumpy, "they must think Zoo Time is being filmed!"
Before DD could reply he noticed his reflection in a mirror, and he let out a loud scream as he noticed that somebody had painted a smiley face on him in biro. Big Jones and all the boys on the bus were in fits of laughter, and passers by were just amazed by what they were witnessing as DD was screaming at all the boys trying to find out who had done this to him. The main one he was blaming was Stumpy as he was the only one he knew that had a pen, and he was the first to remark that it made him look better as it was hiding part of his face.
"You wait," he said trying to wash his face and talk at the same time. "I'll have you all back."

As the bus pulled into London, King Will asked the driver to take them as close to Westminster as possible as that was where the rally was due to start from, but on getting to Westminster they were met with a large police presence and were informed that they could not go near Downing Street as it was off limits and anyone attempting to go there would be arrested. There was quite a good attendance and the march started at around half past ten and went around the city fairly peacefully, with miners from all over the country from South Wales to Durham, Yorkshire and Kent displaying their various banners, and was also supported by other trade unions not affiliated to the Miners' Union. At one point Alfie and Big Jones decided to carry their colliery banner so they tapped the flag bearers on each side on the shoulder and took the flag pole and started to carry on marching through the city.
After about a hundred yards Big Jones shouted across to Alfie
"Do you think the boys are talking funny?"
"No," replied Alfie, "I think they've had a few pints."
"Don't be daft," said Jones, as he glanced up at the banner to discover to his horror that they were carrying the Durham banner. When they did find their own boys they were telling them what had happened, when DD remarked, "Well didn't you tell by the weight of the flag?"
"What do you mean" said Jones.
"Well," DD responded, "the image on our flag is taken off a photo of you, so by the size on that head it must be a fair weight."
The rest of the march was fairly uneventful with the police closing the entrances to Downing Street and Fleet Street so no protesters could get down there, and Whitehall heavily guarded with a lot of police on

horseback.

One of the horseback police was a female officer.Stumpy noticed that the horse was perspiring heavily and he decided to point this out to the officer saying, "You should take that horse to the stables the way it's panting and sweating, the horse needs water."
To which the officer replied in a sarcastic voice, "If you spent eight hours between my legs boy, you would be panting and sweating worse than the horse." And as everybody in earshot started to laugh she dug her spurs into the horse and rode off back into the crowd and out of sight leaving Stumpy for the first time in his life lost for words.

As the day came to an end the crowd filtered off to climb on to their various buses for the long journey home to various parts of the country. The boys were soon aboard the bus back to South Wales and were soon heading down the M4,when Colin Asthma and Big Jones decided to try to get Dai Rugby to ask the bus driver to stop of somewhere to have some food and wanted Dai to pay for it out of the money that he had left over.
"Come on Dai," said Jones, "look at all the empty seats on the bus; you must have some money left over because some of the boys didn't turn up."
"Yes," said Dai, "but I must hand all left over money into the lodge treasurer when we get back."
"Why?" said DD, "King Will and the rest of his Muppets stayed in London. They won't know if nobody says anything, and we're all starving because we couldn't afford no food in London."
"But you could afford to go into a pub instead."
"But we were asking the locals to support us in our struggle against this government, not enjoying ourselves, and we had to have a pint not to seem ignorant," said DD.

The bus carried on out of London and on to the motorway with the chorus of "We want food, we want food" coming from all parts of the bus, to which Dai tried to turn a deaf ear, until a voice from somewhere up the back shouted, "What's the matter Dai? You're scared to spend the money unless you ask King Will, or are you going to stand on the wallet at the next meeting so that you can see over the table?"
This seemed to do the trick as Dai came storming out of his seat screaming, "Driver take us to Chepstow, I know a place where we can have some food."
"Good speech, Dai," came the mystery voice, and brought a loud cheer from everybody on the bus .The driver as instructed pulled off the motorway as ordered and Dai directed him to a car park where all

the boys got off.
"Come on, driver," said Dai, "you're coming with us." Dai led the boys out of the car park and about 200 yards down the road crossed over and went down a side street and into a pub.
"Come on then Dai spend a few bob; after all we've been out all day and if the rest of the boys couldn't be bothered to get out of bed it's not our fault."
"Well said Jones" said his side kick Alfie, "buy the boys a pint."
"O.K.," said Dai, "landlord give me twenty four pints."

As the boys were given their beer they decided that as it was a nice evening that they would take the drinks into the beer garden at the rear of the pub. The boys continued to wind Dai up and by now he was starting to come around to their way of thinking that if they were the only boys to turn up then they deserved to have something out of it.
"Landlord," said Dai starting to sound like King Will's clones, "Where's the nearest place where we can get some food?" "There's a fish and chip shop about 50 yards down the road. I think that's the only place open at this time of day," he replied.
"Right," said Dai, "who wants what? The lodge is paying so come on let me know what you want." "Who's going to go then?" said Stumpy,
"Not you anyway; you haven't moved since we got here," said Colin Asthma.
"Shut up, boy," replied Stumpy.
"Ill go," said Buster, "if Dai and Stumpy go, they won't be able to see over the counter."
"Good thinking boy," said Big Jones taking the last drop out of his pint glass,and already looking for a refill.

After what seemed an age Dai and Buster returned with their arms full of newspapers containing what seemed like an endless supply of vinegar soaked fish and chips,
"Dig in quick boys before the big boy comes back," said Buster noticing that Big Jones was not sitting at the table.
"Where's the big boy gone then?" said Dai Rugby.
"In the toilet," said Stumpy. "He won't be long when he smells the food."
"No he'll eat the paper as well if you let him," said DD as he tore open the package that was thrown at him. Big Jones returned from the toilet clutching a fresh pint in his large hand.
"Where did you get that boy?" all the boys seemed to say at the same time.
"I got talking to some people in the bar and I was telling them where

we were from, and why we were here and they said they wanted to make a donation to the strike fund. Then one of them said his father was a miner, so they all got together and made a collection for us."

"You sure about that," said Stumpy through a mouthful of fish and chips.

"Yes the barman was filling up a couple of jugs for us as I left the bar."

As Big Jones was talking amongst all noises coming from hungry mouths the barman emerged carrying two jugs of beer.

"Here you are boys," he said, "some of the regulars have chipped in for you to have a drink on them."

As the boys were trying to eat and thank the barman at the same time there was what sounded like something landing on paper? As he looked down DD noticed the contents of a bird's stomach spread out all over Stumpy's chips like a line of salad cream. Stumpy neither saw or heard this and continued to hungrily scoff the food into his mouth. DD was just about to warn him not to eat anymore when he had a flash back to the toilet on the motorway and the smiley face that was painted on him that he blamed Stumpy for. As he motioned to big Jones he pointed to the white pattern that the bird had left on Stumpy's chips and putting a finger to his mouth he silently urged the big boy to remain silent, thinking that this was payback time for earlier in the day.

Stumpy meanwhile was greedily stuffing the fish and chips into his mouth as if it was the first meal he had for weeks.

"Take your time boy," said Big Jones, "you're eating that like your are in the Last Supper,"he said trying not to look at what the bird had left on the chips.

"He's old enough to have been at the Last Supper" said Colin Asthma as he also had to hold back his own laughter.

As he returned from the toilet Buster, one of the comedians in the group, made a remark that it was like walking into a chimps' tea party, when he looked across at Stumpy and was just about to make a smart remark when he noticed the extra portion on Stumpy's chips.

"How have you got more than we have?" he said trying to stifle his laughter.

"What you mean?" said Stumpy.

As the boys tried to make signals to Buster to keep quiet it was too late as Stumpy looked down at the paper nestling on his lap and for the first time he saw what everybody else had seen and let him carry on eating. With a scream he threw his fish and chips across the table at DD who by now was almost choking with laughter.

"That's your lot," he said angrily shoving his chair back and jumping to is feet.

Everybody on the table was now laughing as much as DD who they thought was going to burst a blood vessel.
"Never mind Stumpy," said Big Jones, "at least you had some flavour on your chips.Dai rugby forgot to put vinegar on mine."
"Never mind," said Colin Asthma, "it could have been worse."
"How could it have been worse?" said Stumpy who was now starting to feel sorry for himself.
"Well it could have been my chips."
"You wait I'll have you all back," said Stumpy.
"Payback time," said Lou, "maybe it was one of the pigeons the bloke in the club was talking about to me last week; that'll teach you to be clever with me in future."
"DD was the first to see what landed on your food," said Big Jones.
"Aye," said Colin Asthma, "he had a bird's eye view."
This again led to more laughter from the boys, and increased Stumpy's anger.
"Don't forget to keep quiet about who bought the food and beer," said Dai Rugby. "King Will will have me locked up if he finds out about this."
"What do you mean?" quipped Big Jones as quick as a flash, "does that mean he'll make you do a bit of bird?" After all that had happened the boys all decided to stay on in the pub and managed to persuade Dai Rugby to buy two more jugs of beer and they started a sing song in the bar and the locals all duly joined in; Stumpy even gave a song.
"What are you going to sing?" asked Big Jones.
"The pigeon song" quipped DD, as Stumpy got up to cheers from all in the bar, and the evening was made complete when the barman decided to give the boys another jug of beer on the house.
As the boys eventually left the bar they all promised to come back after the strike to repay the locals and the barman for their kindness and hospitality.

Back on the bus Dai Rugby tried his best to ask the boys not to say anything about the food and jugs of beer to King Will, but although his mouth was moving no words were coming out "You're like a goldfish, Dai," said Colin Asthma.
"Yes," said Big Jones, "If King Will finds out you spent money from the funds on the boys you'll have to move faster than that bird that got friendly with Stumpy's chips."
The entire journey back was pretty quiet as most of the boys were sleeping almost as soon as the bus got to the motorway. When the bus got back the boys all got off on their different stops and went home

with memories of a day they will remember for a long time.
As Big Jones remarked to DD as they walked across the field which was a shortcut to their houses, "We got no money, boy, but we can still have some fun, they can't take that off us."
"No but I bet Stumpy wishes somebody took that birds bowels off his chips!",quipped DD.

Chapter 5

The following morning they had to go to the community centre where there was a meeting to let everybody know what the next moves in the strike were going to be. As the boys who went up to London came to the hall, some were looking the worse for wear after the journey and the refreshments they had on the way back, with Dai Rugby telling them "Keep your mouths shut now boys or there will be trouble."
Although there was not a lot said to anybody who was not on the bus everybody seemed to know about what had happened to Stumpy's fish and chips, although nobody was admitting to saying anything. It was Jamie, who was not on the bus, who made the first remark when he asked Stumpy if he had enjoyed the extra flavour on the chips.
"I would have put vinegar on mine," he said, "but you've always been a bit odd."
"Not odd enough to have been married five times," replied Stumpy, with a smile as he said it, and thinking that it was the first time he had seen Jamie stuck for words as everybody in earshot started to laugh.
The outcome of the meeting was that picketing was to be increased and some of the places were to be power stations and pits in England, and volunteers were wanted to go to Oxford on that weekend to picket the Didcot power station where a minibus would be provided and they would be able to stay in one of the colleges which were sponsored by the unions. Big Jones, Alfie, Stumpy, DD and Colin Asthma were amongst the first to volunteer, and they were asked to go on the Tuesday morning and to take some warm clothes as they would be doing a round the clock picket on the power station at Didcot.

On the Tuesday morning the minibus picked the boys up at six in the morning, and was driven by Jamie.
"Must be on a good thing," said Stumpy as he got on the minibus, "we don't see you often."
"All my work is done undercover looking after you lot," came the reply.
"How long will we be on this bus for boy?" said Big Jones.
"Don't know," said Jamie. "I've never been there before, all I got is

the directions off King Will and you all know what he's like."
"I'll get you there," came a voice from the back of the bus. "I was a navigator in the army." It was the Dwarf.
"Who woke you up?" said Colin Asthma.
"I wasn't sleeping, and I am the only one with army training. How do you think I got out of the jungle in Malaya?"
"Pretty quick with that farmer chasing you after you shot his donkey, I suppose," came a quip from DD.
"Pity I didn't have my gun now," said the Dwarf.
"Aye," said Big Jones, "you could have shot that bird for Stumpy last week!"
"I'll shoot you if I get a chance big fella," mumbled Stumpy grinding his teeth as he spoke.
Eventually the minibus pulled up outside Smith house in Oxford, and the boys all jumped out and all looked at the building that was to be their home for the next weekend.
"It looks like a haunted house," said Dai Fine man.
"Good," said Stumpy, "Phil the half man half monster can haunt it for us."
"Don't be nasty" said Big Jones, "but it's right, we all know he's the ugliest man in the world, I've got a photo of him on my mantelpiece to keep the kids away from the fire." But although they didn't know at the time it would be their home for a lot longer than the weekend.
As they walked into the building they were met by a young man of about twenty years of age, who spoke with a heavy Scottish accent and said his name was Ronnie, and he explained that he would be looking after them, and he offered them a meal and some tea or coffee. As they were all quite hungry they accepted his offer and were amazed when he came out with a huge plate of cauliflower cheese and chilli beans. As the boys were eating the food Jamie made a comment on how good the food was and did he cook it himself.
"Yes I did but don't get too carried away because that's all that I can cook: so you will soon get fed up with the same thing, unless one of you can cook."
"You look like someone who likes his food," said the Scotsman looking at Big Jones.
"He'd eat you if you stood still long enough," said DD.
"Anyway there's a canteen that the students use and my girlfriend is one of the cooks there, so I will ask her if she will keep any food that is left over for you. Only thing is we've only got a few sleeping bags for you boys so it will be first come first served. The rest will have to make do with blankets on the floor.
"Is there a bar here?" asked Stumpy
"Yes, there is, and there are a few pubs in the town that the students use which are pretty good. If you like I will take you there."

That was what all the boys were waiting to hear and quick as a flash they were all changed and heading out of the door. On the way to the bar there was a lot of talk about who should get the first round when DD suggested that they should all put £5 in the kitty and that then there would be no arguments about who should be paying, which came as a surprise to the boys as Stumpy said, “That is the only sensible thing you have said since this strike began,” causing a lot of laughter and some choice words from DD, but it was all taken in good heart.

In the bar, Ronnie the Scotsman told the boys to wait outside while he went inside to make sure he could take the boys inside. When he returned he was with a large coloured girl who he said was the head of the Students’ Union and it was O.K. to use the bar for the time that they would be in Oxford. The girl explained that she was from South Africa and she was studying politics and that her name was Julia. “If you have any problems here just see Ronnie and he will contact me and I will sort it out for you,” she said. “If you go into the Students Union the students have made a collection for you and there are some drinks there for you all. The boys did not need to be told twice and were heading for the bar when Jamie stopped them in their tracks saying, “Don’t forget boys we need a rota for our picketing duties in the morning.”

“How about we put all the names in a hat and pick out who does the first one and we can sort out the rest in the morning,” said Big Jones. “If we’re going to do that let’s use DD’s hat as it is the biggest one here and we can get more into it,” said Colin Asthma as Stumpy spat out a mouthful of his beer over Alfie as he laughed out loud.
“Why don’t we just use your mouth?” came the reply from DD but it was too late the damage was done and Alfie was left with a wet shirt. After a few drinks and some more debating about who should do the first picketing duties they decided that DD’s suggestion was the best option as nobody was going to volunteer. So Jamie got a glass and put all the names on to paper and then carefully cutting the paper into squares each name was carefully put into it and he invited Ronnie to pick the names out. Ronnie stood up and amid total silence he started to take the pieces of paper out of the glass,
“The first name out is Alfie,” he said.
“Just my luck, we get free beer and I’ve got to get up at 4 in the morning.”
“Quiet now,” said Ronnie, “we need a partner for you, so the next name is . . .”
He paused to open the crumpled piece of paper and announced, “The

next name is Stumpy."
"Fix," said Stumpy. "I bet you only put our names into the glass."
"It could be worse, it could have been my name," said DD.

As the evening went on the boys were all given 5 free pints of beer which they were all grateful for and they managed to keep most of the kitty money for the following night. Jamie came back off the telephone to announce that the first picketing duties were to take place at a power station about 5 miles from where they were staying, and Ronnie was to organise a van to take the first lot of boys to do the first picket duty and he announced that he would drive the van himself as the van that Jamie had driven them up in had to go back in the morning, and he would be at Smith house at 4-30 in the morning.
"So whoever is doing the first shift had better be heading back to the digs to get some sleep." But Alfie and Stumpy just ignored him. As usual the evening ended with a sing-song and even the students got involved as Stumpy and Dai Fine man again led the singing.

The night was a successful night for the boys from the valleys as the students were calling them, and some lasting friendships were starting to develop even in these early days. The only blot on the night was when DD thought a student was trying to mimic his accent and he was threatening to knock his teeth down his throat.
"Cool down," said Alfie, "whenever you have a drink you think you're Two-can Van Damme just like Big Jones. The boy is only trying to be friendly, and these people have been with us all night."
DD finally calmed down and accepted the student's apology and the singing carried on until the bar closed around midnight.
"So much about going back to the digs early," said Alfie.

On the way back to Smith house the boys had to pass down a cobble stone street which was lit by a row of lamp posts, under one of the lamp posts there was a skip and on the top was a baby's cot mattress,
"I'm having that," said Stumpy. "I'm not going to sleep on a cold floor."
And in a flash Stumpy was in the skip and had the mattress out of there.
"It'll be like sleeping in the house with a small mattress" said DD.
"All you need now is someone to make you tea in the morning, and help you get dressed," said Colin Asthma following on from DD's remark through Stumpy's grumbling and some chuckling from the boys.
"We'll see how funny you lot are in the morning when I wake you lot up before I go anywhere," said Stumpy.

The morning seemed to come as soon as the boys shut their eyes when a long haired student came into the room where the boys were sleeping and woke Alfie and Stumpy with some difficulties,
"What's up?" said Stumpy, "I've only just got to sleep," through half opened eyes.
"It's 4 o'clock. Do you want a cup of tea before you go?" said the student.
"I don't drink tea," said Alfie.
"You can have coffee if we've got any left," said the student as he walked away into the small room that they were using as a kitchen. A few minutes later he returned with two cups which looked like they had not been washed since they had been made. As the student left the room Alfie said to Stumpy
"Look at these cups Stumpy. I would rather drink out of a hospital sample bottle and that student looks like the last bath he had the mid -wife did it."
Stumpy took a gulp of his tea and immediately spat it out screeching to Alfie, "I think it was a sample in there. I have never tasted anything like that in my life; it was worse than the tea in the pit canteen."

Before any more could be said Ronnie pulled up in the van at 4.30 as he had promised.
"Do me a favour," said Stumpy, "can you get me a glass of cold water?"
He gladly did so, and as Stumpy got up to go he walked over to where DD was sleeping and turning to Ronnie he said, "You had better get the van started if you want to keep it in one piece," and as Ronnie and Alfie got to the top of the stairs he threw water over DD's head waking him up with a howl like a banshee, and as Stumpy ran down the stairs with what he described in the van as a blue flash and a smell of burning rubber, everybody in the room was woken up with DD screaming down the stairs at Stumpy and telling him that he was going to rip his head off when he got his hands on him, and Stumpy shouting back , "Now it's not so funny that I had to get up, is it boy?"

On the way to the power station where they were to spend the next 6 hours picketing, the two miners and the Scottish student had a chuckle about how Stumpy had woken his sleeping colleague with a water bath and what would happen when they got back.
"I'll give him a flying head butt to the knee cap if he starts," said Stumpy, which was one of his favourite sayings.

As the van approached the power station Ronnie explained that the students had built some temporary shelter for them and that some

local people had offered to provide refreshments for them.
"All I want is an aspirin for my banging head," said Stumpy.
"With a head that size you might need a box of aspirin; it must be like a thunderstorm," said Alfie with a sarcastic tone to his voice.
"Anyway you don't deserve any sympathy, the way you were knocking back the free beer last night."
"I had to have a drink to relax my vocal cords before I could sing because none of you lot was going to give a song," replied the silver fox.

When they got to the power station Ronnie explained that they were not allowed to go on to the power station grounds and here the students had built the shelter was as close they could go without trespassing on to the power station grounds.
"O.K. this is it," said Ronnie, "some of the locals said they will organise some coffee and sandwiches for you and there is a fire station just up the hill and I will ask them if they can help you in some way."
"What time do the coal wagons start to come in?" asked Alfie.
"All depends, we have not been keeping checks and the manager of the power station has not been very helpful as you can understand."
"Is there another entrance to the station?" asked Stumpy.
"Yes there is another entrance about 500 yards up the hill by the fire station but at the moment we think they are only using this entrance, we spoke to one of the union reps, but they said they could not promise anything, and confirmed that the manager was not very union friendly at the moment but they would do their best, but I will go to the fire station and ask them there to keep a look out for us as the boys there have said they will help you in any way they can, and the union rep there is a Scotsman I can talk to him."

As Ronnie pulled off in the van Alfie noticed that Stumpy's mood had started to improve although he was still complaining about how he thought the names in the hat were fixed but he seemed to cheer when Alfie mentioned what he had done to DD before they had left the digs.
"Good enough for him; he thinks because I'm small he can bully me but I'll smash him in the kneecaps if he starts on me."
"But he says he was a boxer so you had better watch yourself Stumpy," replied Alfie,
"Boxer?he was the only boxer to have handles on his shorts, and a cauliflower backside," replied Stumpy with a smile on his face which seemed to show that he had forgotten about his hangover from the previous night.
"You know they used to call him the canvas back kid because he was

so bad that he was lucky to come second in his fights."
."Well I would still watch yourself."
As Alfie was talking there suddenly was the sound of a lorry in the distance and as the two picketing miners looked up the road they could see in the distance a six wheel lorry heading down the hill in the direction of the power station.
"This is it the first one of the day," said Stumpy, "come on son let's go and stop it."

He started to get ready to try to go and stop the wagon and ask the driver for some support for the striking miners.
As the lorry got closer Stumpy stepped nervously out on to the road off the grass verge followed closely by his mate Alfie.
"Hold on Stumpy," said Alfie, "he doesn't look like he's going to stop; get out of the way!"
And it seemed that he was right as instead of slowing down the lorry seemed to continue to come at them not appearing to slow down at all. Suddenly Stumpy could see that however much he waved his arms the lorry was not going to slow down and Stumpy had no choice but to dive back on to the grass verge losing his balance and falling flat on his back causing a snigger from Alfie.
"What you laughing at? I was almost flattened into the tarmac! Handy mate you are: all you can do is laugh. "Well I can't see the funny side but at least I tried."
"I shouted to you to move but I must have on your deaf side again," said Alfie still with a grin on his face. "When he comes back out I'm having him," said the silver fox still rubbing his leg and complaining about how he nearly broke his back for the miners' cause.

Chapter 6

As the two boys patiently waited for the lorry to come out from the power station there was another rumbling of an engine in the distance and then over the brow of the hill came the second wagon of the day carrying more coal for the power station furnaces. This time the boys decided to stay on the grass verge and try to stop the lorry in safety. As the wagon came within eyesight the two boys frantically started to wave their arms trying to catch the driver's attention. Gradually the wagon seemed to slow down and as it got closer the boys could see that it was slowly coming to a halt and as it got close enough for the boys to smell the diesel fumes it came to a complete halt and the driver wound the window down to talk to the two picketing miners, but they did not seem to be having any success as the driver explained that he had orders off his boss that the load had to be delivered and although he felt sorry for what was happening to the miners he could not afford to lose his job. All the boys could do was agree that they did not want people to lose their jobs but if the miners were beaten then who would be next on the conservative hit list?

As the morning seemed to be coming to a dead end the two miners were starting to wonder if there was any use in them coming up here to try to get some support, but as they were sitting in the makeshift shelter there was a sound of voices outside. As the two men got up to go and look outside there was a young woman standing there with what looked like a picnic basket balancing on the handlebars of the bike that she was riding. As she rested the bike against the shelter she took the holdall off her back and put the basket on to the ground and removed parcels of food and a flask of coffee for the boys which they were more than happy to take.

"This is from the local women's action support group which has been set up with help from the students at the university so I hope that you are hungry," explained the woman who looked too young to be involved in a dispute of this nature.

"Are we hungry, I think Stumpy could eat a photo of the Last Supper," said Alfie, as Stumpy was already ripping the paper off the sandwiches.

"Why are you down here when the coal lorries are going in and out of the top gates?" she asked as the boys were munching away on the sandwiches that she had brought to them.

"We were told that the power station manager had said that the top gates would be closed and the only entrance to be used would be these ones," said Stumpy as he stopped eating long enough to answer the question.

"Well they are using the top gates because I've just passed there and a lorry almost knocked me off my bike," she said.

"I bet it's the same bloke who almost turned me into a yard of tarmac this morning" said Stumpy, as the young woman looked at him wondering what he meant.

"Come on Stumpy" said Alfie.

"We had better get up there and try to stop them."

"Hang on," said the silver fox.

"This is the first food I've had since last night, and anyway the van will be here before long and we can get Ronnie to take us up there."

"What time is the van due to come for us?" asked Alfie,

"Well he said about 2 o'clock but he might have had his watch on Scottish time so you never know what time he might be here," said Alfie.

"Well I am going home now so do you know the college phone number and I will phone them for you," said the young woman,

"No we don't know how to get in touch with him," said Alfie who like Stumpy was trying to talk and eat at the same time.

Just as the girl on the bike disappeared over the brow of the hill there came the sound of an old diesel engine coming in the opposite direction which the boys were both hoping would be Ronnie their new Scottish friend, and their prayers were soon answered as sure enough a blue transit van appeared and pulled up alongside the two men and a broad Scottish accent was asking them if they were all right as he stepped out of the driver's seat. Stumpy and Alfie soon filled Ronnie in on the events of the day and he seemed as surprised as they were as he thought that the power station had agreed to only use the bottom gate, but said that he would try and get in touch with somebody from the union at the power station to try and get somebody to explain the reason why they opened the top gates after it was agreed to keep the top gate shut.

As the three men made their way back to the college where they were staying Ronnie told the two boys that the rest of the boys were all in the town with buckets trying to get a collection to help the miners fight to keep the pits open and save their jobs,
"How is DD" asked Alfie, "is he still going to tear Stumpy's head off or has he cooled down?"
"Last time I saw him he was standing in the town with a pile of leaflets in his hand and didn't look too happy with life," said Ronnie.
"He's never happy," said Stumpy, "but I'll soon cheer him up when I give him the crust off one of the sandwiches I kept for him," said Stumpy with a huge grin on his face.

The van arrived back at the college and Ronnie dropped the two boys off and went to park the van up for the night.
"How did it go then boy?" said Big Jones, as soon as they came up the stairs and into the room which was home to them for their stay in Oxford.
"All right except that Stumpy almost killed himself," said Alfie.
"What you mean?" said the grey haired one, "that lorry driver nearly turned me into a part of the road, but I was too quick for him."
As Stumpy recalled the story of how he almost wrote a lorry off Ronnie came into the room.
"I've been in touch with my mate in the fire station and he told me that the power station did use the top gates, and that he heard that they will continue to do so for as long as there will be a picket line there."
"What can we do about this then? We can't let them get away with this," said Colin Asthma taking a large puff on his inhaler as he always did when he got worked up.

"I'll go and phone King Will and see if he can get more boys up here so that we can man both gates," said Jamie.
"Great," said Ronnie, "but I have got some news for you which might cheer you up," he said with a smile on his face. "The boys at the fire station are organising a stag party on Friday night at the fire station club for one of their boys who is getting married, and they asked if you boys would like to go."
"As far as I know the power station have not been having any deliveries on weekends so you can all go if you want to, and they have made a collection for you to have a drink or two, so let me know if you want to go and I will sort it out for you."
"If you want to go I will phone King Will and ask him if I can use some of the picketing money I have got left from the three boys who didn't come up here, and can the minibus that is taking you home on Saturday morning come a bit later for you, but you'll have to phone your wives because I'm not taking the blame for you lot not getting home on time," said Jamie.

As the boys talked among themselves there seemed to be no doubt that they all wanted to go to the stag do. "We should go boys said Alfie because after all these firemen said they wanted to help us."
"And the free beer sounds good too, so I think we should go," said DD.
So it was decided that Ronnie should tell the firemen that the boys were grateful for their offer and that they would like to come to the stag party. Jamie came back off the phone and told the boys that King Will had said he could use the money he had left for the boys and he would sort the minibus out and that he would try to get some more men up to help with the picketing of the power station since both entrances were being used. The next two days passed off fairly uneventfully and much the same as the previous two days with the manager of the power station refusing to Co-operate with the striking miners and refusing to meet with anybody associated with any industrial action. As the week went by the boys kept themselves busy by doing their best at the power station, with no success as they tried to get the lorry drivers to stop.

The few who did stop all had the same story that they had been told that their jobs depended on them making these deliveries, and if they would not do as they were told there was a lot of drivers waiting to take their place, but all the boys knew that they were being well paid to cross the picket lines and in most cases they were told by some of the drivers that as the strike was classed as unofficial and was not recognised by all the unions that they had no right to ask them to stop going through the gates, plus the fact that some of the drivers were self-employed and not part of any union did not help. The other thing that all striking miners found hard to come to terms with were the amount of lorries that were taking coal to power stations and other places that appeared to have no road tax, and some appeared to seem un roadworthy, but the police managed to turn a blind eye to these things.

One day 2 police officers turned up at the bottom gates where Big Jones and DD were trying to stop the coal lorries going into the power station and explained that there had been a complaint that some of the picketing miners were hurling stones at the lorries as they passed by without stopping but after a short talk to the 2 boys they seemed happy to accept that the boys seemed genuine enough. As the police officers talked to the boys one of them said that his grandfather was a Welshman and that he also worked in the coal mines and that he had a lot of sympathy for the miners' cause, but like a lot of people had also said he did not agree with the way that the strike was being handled in the way that the miners in Nottingham were being denied a vote, and the boys had to agree that it split the union and made the strike a lot harder. Big Jones came up with a comment that he would like to get a red hot poker and push it up Maggie Thatcher's backside cold end first." "Why cold end first?" the officer enquired, with a puzzled look on his face.
"So she would burn her hand when she pulled it out," replied the big fella which seemed to bring a smile to the faces of both officers.

As the night of the stag party came the boys were told that a minibus would be sent to pick them up from outside the pub down the road from where they were staying to take them to the fire station club at 7 0'clock so they all would have time to get ready if they were on the picket lines or doing other things. As promised the minibus turned up 5 minutes early and they all climbed aboard and the driver set off to the fire station club with all the boys in good spirits and looking forward to a night out, the first in a long time for most of them, apart from Colin Asthma who according to Stumpy was out every night when he was home calling bingo or other committee duties that he could get. When they got to the fire station club there were double doors as you went in where there was a table where two men were sitting to make sure that nobody entered the club who was not a member or was not invited. As the first man rose to his feet the boys could see from his size and his broken nose that he was not the sort of man to argue with. Jamie stepped forward and explained that the boys were invited to a stag party and that it had been organised by Ronnie the Scottish student.

The man put out a hand the size of a bear and told the boys to go into the hall and that they were expected, as the boys moved into the hall Stumpy heard a voice calling from a small bar to the left of the hall and when he looked it was the girl who had brought the sandwiches for him and Alfie on the first day they were there, so he went in to talk to her and the girl standing with her and offered them a drink which they refused as they were going. As the rest of the boys went into the hall they were told that there was a buffet laid on and that the cans of beer and lager were free but they would have to pay for any shorts.
"Stumpy will feel at home then," said Colin Asthma taking the chance to have a go at his mate for a change. "Shut up, and go and see if they will be playing bingo so you can call the numbers," came the reply as Stumpy came in behind them with Alfie.
"Shut up you two", said DD, "and go and get some drinks."
"First time Stumpy has been first to go to the bar since Winston Churchill was boy," shouted the dwarf who had already had got a seat and was waiting for his drink.
"Who's working you," said Big Jones, "you're the same as Stumpy, and you need a map to find the bar."
"At least I can read a map: how do you think I got out of the jungle in Malaya during my army days," said the dwarf.
"Very quickly, with a farmer chasing you," said DD which caused a lot of laughter from the entire group of boys."
"I got some drinks," said Big Jones, "but I didn't know how long you two would be so one of you will have to go to the bar a get yours."

As Stumpy and Alfie went to the bar they did not know what the other boys were told about the drinks, so as the young girl behind the bar asked Stumpy what he wanted he asked for two lagers.
"Are cans all right?" she asked. "They are cold."
To which Stumpy replied that cans would be fine. As the girl came back with the cans Stumpy asked how much they were.
"Free" replied the girl.
"No, I only asked for two," said Stumpy.
"The cans are free for you," she said again. By this time Alfie had understood what the girl meant and as he looked across at the other boys he could see that they all could hear what was happening and were all in fits of laughter.
Before Stumpy could say another word the girl who could also see the funny side of things said, "The drinks are free, as in you don't pay for them."

Looking around at his mates Stumpy could see them all laughing, and just thanked the girl and walked from the bar to where all of the boys were sitting down and laughing, along with some of the other people who were sitting close enough to see and hear what was happening. "First time you've been stuck for words since that time you called a false house in the club," said Big Jones.

The evening carried on with a lot more banter and as the firemen who had organised the stag party came in they were told that there was a stripper booked for later on but the boy who was getting married did not know and there would a surprise later on. The hall soon filled up and the firemen quickly had the young groom and his best man handcuffed together and nobody seemed to know where the key was. As the boys started enjoying themselves they started to get to know some of the firemen as if they were long lost friends and were soon swapping stories of previous stag parties they had all been to.

As the time came for the stripper to come on there was an air of excitement around the hall and as she came on the stage there was a loud cheer and a few people moved as close to the stage as they could. As the stripper got into her routine she came off the stage and pulled DD up on to the stage where she sat him down on a chair she had been using, where she sat down on his lap and put one of her nipples in his mouth and then pulled it out quickly causing his two false teeth in the front to come flying out and sliding to the front of the stage where the dwarf was sitting and he quickly grabbed the teeth and put them into his pocket before DD could see where they went, this caused a lot of laughter among the crowd, but DD did not see the funny side and was screaming at everyone in sight but nobody owned up to knowing where they were, and if he had known where they were the dwarf would have been in big trouble.
"Sit down and have a pint and keep your mouth shut and nobody will notice," said Colin Asthma,
"I'll come back in the morning to see if the cleaner has found them," said Jamie, "if you don't find them tonight."
To which Stumpy said, "It'll take more than one woman to pick those teeth up," which made DD's temper worse than it already was. As all this was going on the dwarf managed to pass the teeth to Big Jones who was sitting next to DD and when DD was looking on the floor for his teeth Big Jones dropped the teeth into Stumpy's glass.
"Come on boys it's no good arguing: let's have another drink and when the stripper's finished her act I'll ask for the lights to be put on and we can all look for the teeth."

DD grumpily agreed and as the boys drank their beer Big Jones managed to attract the attention of most of the boys on the tables and made eyes towards Stumpy as he lifted his glass to drink his beer, and

as he came to the bottom of the glass a set of dentures dropped in to his mouth almost chocking the silver fox.
"I knew you had them," said DD trying to get at Stumpy and grab his teeth at the same time.
"It wasn't me I thought that Jaws was coming at me," said Stumpy.
"Never mind now boy just put the teeth back in before you lose them again."

All through this the stripper was still doing her act and she wanted somebody else to get up on the stage with her, but nobody was willing to go until the crowd started to shout for the groom to get on the stage along with the best man who he was still handcuffed to. As he was protesting he did not want to go on the stage especially in handcuffs a member of the crowd who had been sitting quietly by the front of the stage decided to get up. The man appeared to be in his late forties and one of the men by the table said that he was a fireman and a bit of a character and had a cigarette in the corner of his mouth which he refused to remove and no matter what the stripper tried he appeared to be totally uninterested which was not going down well with the stripper. But all the time the firemen in the hall were to shouting to him and egging him on, when he suddenly jumped off the chair causing the stripper to move sharply out of his way, and he started to remove his shirt and undo his trousers leaving them fall around his ankles to reveal a bright red pair of French knickers and matching suspender belt and stockings leaving the stripper looking on in amazement but knowing that she had been set up.

The stag party was still going on when the minibus arrived for the boys to go back to the college and as the boys left the club DD was still grumbling about who took his teeth and when he found out he was going to tear his head off his shoulders, when Big Jones shouted from the back of the bus.
"The state on you boy you got a job to stand never mind tear somebody's head off!"
As DD turned to answer he just fell down on to the seat in fits of laughter as Big Jones was sitting there with the red suspender belt around his neck. As the minibus made its way back to the college there was still the odd mention of the teeth but the sight of the big fella with the suspenders around his neck appeared to have defused what could have been a tricky situation.

When the minibus pulled up outside the college Stumpy was first out and quickly ran up the stairs so no one else could take his precious cot mattress and by the time it took Big Jones to get DD out of the bus as by now he was sleeping and up the stairs Stumpy was on his mattress

and sound asleep which is how he stayed until the morning despite numerous attempts to interrupt his sleep.
"Leave him there, if he wakes up now all he will do is start to sing and then nobody will get to sleep," said Colin Asthma. And with DD also snoring the rest of the boys were soon fast asleep. As the morning came Colin Asthma was as usual the first to wake and he went over to the small table in the corner to make a cup of tea and as he put the kettle to boil he looked around at all his colleagues in various contorted shapes on the floor, and Stumpy on his mattress, and Big Jones still with the suspenders around his neck and thought to himself that if he told the rest of the boys back home they would have had him committed. As the kettle came to the boil he reached over the table to find the cleanest cup he could amongst a mountain of dirty crockery when he heard a voice saying,"Two sugars for me," and as he looked around he could see Stumpy still lying on his mattress with one eye open and his hand outstretched. "My mouth is like that strippers cod piece," he said bringing a smile to Colin's face as he passed him his tea in a cracked and stained mug.
"How are you feeling?" asked Colin.
"I felt great until I woke up," replied Stumpy, without looking up from under the blanket he had over the mattress he stole from the skip. "And if you want a clean cup you can wash it yourself," he said.

As Stumpy and Colin were drinking their tea Alfie shouted across. "Why don't you two shut up?" and asked Colin the time as he rubbed his eyes and laughed as he caught a glimpse of DD and Big Jones huddled up together and the belt still around his neck.
"He must be taking it home as a present," said Colin Asthma."The time is half past seven, so we had better wake them all up."
As the boys all started to come around Ronnie the Scotsman came in and told them that if they wanted breakfast there was a café just down the road that did good full English or he would make them some bacon and eggs. The thought of eating anything that Ronnie made in the morning made the boys decide to go to the café as they all remembered the breakfast that he made them on the first morning there or as the dwarf called it "bacon and egg soup." So it was decided that it was to be the café. As they entered the café Ronnie told the boys to leave him order as he knew the owner and he might get him to give a discount if they all wanted a breakfast, the only one who declined breakfast was Big Jones who asked if the owner had any fruit. Ronnie came back from the counter and said that they could all have a cup of tea or coffee free of charge providing they all had a breakfast and he had an apple and a glass of water for Big Jones.

The food came to the table and although there were a few hangovers

from the previous night there was no an empty plate to be seen, and as Ronnie went to pay the bill big Lou was trying to get the boys out of the café to get back to the college for the minibus.
"Don't forget now boys what happened last night stays up here," said Alfie.
"Not even about what Big Jones had on," said the dwarf.
"You do and I'll hit you so hard and so far that when you get back your clothes will be out of fashion," said Big Jones.

As the boys headed back to the college all nursing different degrees of hangovers they were all agreed that the night in the firemen's club was the best night they had all had since the strike began and if they came back up again they would all go back and thank them for the hospitality that they were shown.
"It was a good night," said Colin Asthma,
"Yes it was" said Big Jones, "but the same thing happens wherever we go, we have always got to go back a second time."
"Why is that " said Alfie.
"So Stumpy can apologise," replied the big boy.

The journey back to South Wales seemed a long and boring drive as most of the boys were still complaining of sore heads from the night before, but Oddball the driver was in no mood for any sympathy as he told the boys that he had been up since half past four and that he did not have a pint the night before because they wanted to come home a day later to go to a stag party, but he did agree to stop the minibus so that the boys could have a break and stretch their legs, so he stopped off at a farm he noticed on the way up. At the farm the boys went to the farm shop where they bought some tea and coffee and Big Jones bought an apple and an orange and some strawberries for his wife. They also noticed that the farm shop was selling homemade cider and decided that the next time they were passing that they would buy some.

As the minibus came closer to home Jamie once again told the boys that what happened in the club stayed in the club, and they all agreed to say nothing much to the annoyance of the dwarf who had been waiting for years to get something on Big Jones. The minibus dropped the boys off at different places with the dwarf being dropped off last as he lived by the driver, and this made him more miserable than he already was. Big Jones and DD were the first off the bus and as they walked across the field they used as a short cut DD tried to get him to tell what happened the day they walked across there when he had to make a run for it.
"What you mean boy?" asked Big Jones.

"Well Lou said that you were out in the night and you were very quiet and your missus said if you did not behave yourself she would tell him what you did that afternoon."
"Don't listen to Lou you know how he likes to stir things up," said Big Jones, but DD noticed that the big boy went slightly red and seemed to want to change the subject, which made him think that there was more to this, and he was going to find out.

Chapter 7

As he went through the door his wife was waiting for him and told him that she wanted to go shopping and as he protested that he needed a bath and a shave she told him that if he did not take her shopping he would not have any Sunday dinner as she needed a joint of meat so the bath and shave would have to wait. As Big Jones went around the supermarket he followed his wife with a trolley and was told not to throw things into the trolley as he always did as money was tight. At the fresh meat counter there was a queue and his wife took a ticket and took her place in the queue and suddenly he noticed a plate on the counter of off cuts of meat, never a man to let an opportunity go missing the big fella took a piece of meat off the plate and started to happily chew on it.

As he took another piece of meat he spotted his good friend Alfie approaching with his wife and called him over and Alfie to took a piece of meat off the plate, as the two women chatted in the queue Big Jones and Alfie were standing there talking about what the strike had in store for them while still picking pieces of meat off the plate until the two women turned to see what the their husbands were doing , and to their horror all that was left on the plate was a few pieces of fat and a furious shop assistant who was complaining that she had only just put the samples out and that they were there for all the customers and not just to be eaten by the two men, who were both standing there with big smiles on their faces wondering, what all the fuss was about.
"What's her problem boy?" said Big Jones "all you done was take a piece of meat off the plate, you could think that she had to pay for it."
"What you mean me?" said Alfie "I only had one piece, you had the rest."
But they decided to make a quick getaway when they looked at the two wives, who were standing there with faces like thunder, and they knew it was time to go.

The rest of the weekend passed by fairly quickly and soon it was time to go back to Oxford to the picket lines and some peace for Big Jones

and Alfie as their wives were still giving them what for over the meat. When they got back to the college where they were staying Big Jones and Alfie decided to take a walk into the town as they were not needed until the evening. On the way out of the college Alfie noticed an Afro wig lying on the floor just inside the door which he picked up and put into his pocket, and asked if it belonged to anybody and was told that it was there from a fancy dress party on the weekend and it had been left there and nobody wanted it.
"What do you want that for, boy?" said Big Jones.
"I might take it home and wear it in the winter to keep my head warm," he replied, "and it might stop you calling me cue ball head."
Big Jones laughed and said, "A cue ball has got more hair than you!"
As they walked into the town they passed a hairdresser, which was about half full but seemed very busy. Alfie put the wig on and stepped inside and one of the hairdressers stopped what she was doing and looked at him. "Can you give me a trim please?" he asked the girl.

The girl looked at him and replied, "If you don't mind waiting, one of us will see to you when we can."
Quick as a flash Alfie whipped off the wig and said to the girl, "No problem, if I leave it here I can pick it up later on the way back," and walked out of the shop leaving the wig on the chair by the door, much to the amusement of a couple of young boys and a girl who were waiting for their hair to be cut.

When Big Jones and Alfie got back to the college the boys who were not on picket line duty were in the student's union canteen and Stumpy was chatting away to some of the students.
"Looks like the Brain of Britain is giving a lecture to that lot," said Alfie to his mate. "Come on let's go see what he's talking about."
As the two friends made their way over for once Stumpy was talking sense as they were discussing the merits of the strike, and he was putting across the fact that the strike was not about money but was about jobs and if the conservative government beat the miners, then the railways and other seemingly strong unions would be next, and was also telling them about how the power stations had been told to stockpile coal in the event of the strike being an on-going thing. The conversation went on and soon changed to something different when somehow the subject of reincarnation cropped up.
"And what is your opinion on reincarnation" said one of the students, in a slightly foreign accent and looking at Stumpy as he spoke, but he didn't know that he was sitting on the side of his deaf ear, but none the less the answer he got almost made him fall off his chair.
"I don't like powered milk, it gives me heartburn. I'd rather go

without," came the reply.
And as all around him burst out laughing with the exception of the open-mouthed student, Stumpy just sat there with a look of wonder on his face as he asked them all, "What are you all laughing at" But nobody told him, and left him to wonder.

As the evening went on the boys swapped stories of what they got up to during the strike and started to get friendly with the students and found out that most of them were from working class families and had a lot of sympathy for the miners' cause. One of the students pulled a small tin from his pocket and produced what seemed like a roll up cigarette until he lit it and as soon as the first puff of smoke left his lips the smell left nothing to the imagination as to what it was and as he proceeded to pass it around to the other students who in turn took long deep drags and passed it on to the person they were sitting next to, until the reefer came to be passed to the dwarf who shook his head and said politely, "No thank you, them roll-ups are too strong for me. I'll stick to Woodbine."
Which again caused fits of laughter among the boys and the students, with the exception of the dwarf who still did not realise what he had said.

The following morning the four boys who were on picket line duty were woke up at 4.30 by Lenny the chef as he was known due to the fact that he claimed to have been a cook during his time in the army, although the dwarf would argue that he was in the army at the same time and he reckoned that the closest Lenny ever got to cooking was when he had to peel potatoes during his numerous spells in the barrack jail. Lenny would wake the boys who were going on to the early morning picket line duty with either a cup of tea or coffee and a couple of rounds of toast before Jock turned up with the minibus. This particular morning it was quite a cold morning and as Big Jones, Alfie, Stumpy and DD were sitting in the van they were all hoping that whoever was on picket duty throughout the night had kept a fire going for them. As they got closer to the power station they decided that Stumpy and Alfie would go to the top gate and Big Jones and DD would stay at the bottom gate. When they got to the bottom gate they saw that Dai Fine man and his partner had kept the fire going and it was not too cold as Big Jones and DD got out of the van. Dai Fine man told them as he got into the van that it had been quiet all night and the two boys got into the makeshift cabins that had been set up by the gates of the power station at the top and bottom of the hills. The van pulled off up the hill and Alfie and Stump got out and after a quick chat with Jamie and his partner they also saw that they had kept the fire going for them and as the van pulled off they also got into their cabins to wait to see if any coal wagons came to deliver any coal.

It was fairly quiet with just a few cars passing, with sometimes somebody shouting in support and the occasional shout of go back home and do a day's work or similar comments but generally the local people were supportive of the miners.
As the morning drew on the boys kept on topping up the fire with whatever wood was there until the supply of wood that had been collected from the nearby woods started to dwindle down,
"I'm going for walk down the hill to see Big Jones and DD," said Alfie.
"Don't be long then in case I need you," said Stump.
As Alfie started to walk down the hill he took a short cut through the field where he noticed a pile of logs on some waste land, quickly he turned back and as he got back up to the top cabin his mate Stumpy was sitting inside the cabin,
"You weren't long boy," said Stump.
"No," replied Alfie, "I've just found a pile of old logs down by the field, dumped on some waste land," he told his friend.
"If we could get a saw we could saw some up and it would keep the fire going for a long time."
"Wait here I'll go up to the fire station and ask if they can lend us a saw for a couple of hours; it's only just down the road and around the corner and they told us that if we wanted anything to ask them," said Stump, as he set off down the road.

About half an hour later Stumpy turned up with a bow saw on his shoulder.
"Where have you been?" said Alfie. "I thought you had gone back home for a saw."
"Never mind where I've been, let's get one of the boys from down the bottom gate to watch things up here, and we can go and cut some logs so that the fire will keep on burning."
"I'll go down to the bottom gate and get DD or Big Jones to come and watch things up here, or what if I take the saw with me and then I can go straight over to where the logs are with whoever wants to come with me instead of me having to walk up the hill and then back to where the logs are".
"That's the most sensible thing you've said for a long time," said Stumpy
Alfie was already making his way down the hill to the bottom gate with the saw on his shoulder.
"Where you going boy?" said Big Jones as Alfie walked up to the bottom gate.

"I've found a pile of old logs that we can cut up to keep the fire going, so I need a hand to cut them up, before someone else takes them," said Alfie.
"I'll come, I could do with a break from DD moaning all the time," said Big Jones and before DD could complain the two friends were up and going up the hill towards where the logs were.

When they got to where the logs were the two boys decided cut one log up and take it to the gates so that the fires could be kept burning and then Stumpy and DD could go and cut another one, and then if that was enough for the rest of the day they would tell the next lot of boys on the picket line where the logs were and they could go and cut some more and make sure that there was enough for the boys who were there through the night to keep the fire going.

Big Jones and Alfie were soon hard at work cutting the logs and the saw they were given by the firemen seemed pretty sharp considering that it looked a bit out of date.
"Come on boy," said Big Jones as the last of the log was cut into pieces small enough carry, and they went back to the gates where their mates were waiting for them.
As Alfie got back to where Stumpy was waiting for him, Stumpy was sitting by the fire smoking a roll up and drinking tea from the flask that was brought to him by one of the locals. Stumpy went back down the hill to meet DD and about an hour later he came back and told Alfie that they had cut a pile of logs and had hidden them and when the van came to pick them up they could go down to where they were hidden and leave some on each gate to save carrying them and the other boys could do the same and there would always be logs for the fire. When the van came with some more boys to look after the picket lines Alfie and Stumpy told them about the logs they found. They all agreed that it was a good idea to hide the saw so that they didn't have to keep on carrying it up and down the hill, and as they saw the fire burning, and felt the heat of the fire it was decided that when the boys got back to the college that they would pass the word around.

Chapter 8

The collecting of the logs for the fire went on for 2 or 3 weeks and they were quietly starting to disappear when one day as Alfie and Big Jones were walking up to where the logs were they were stopped by two men dressed in grey suits and ties and driving a car with post office telecommunications on the side, and one asked the two boys if they had seen anybody taking any telegraph poles from a nearby field

where they had been left for contractors to erect around the area but most of them are missing. Alfie turned around and tried to conceal his guilt and laughter when Big Jones quick as a flash said, "I've not seen anything but one night last week I saw a lorry down by the waste land and they were putting something on to the back but I couldn't see what it was. How about you, Alfie, have you noticed anything going on?"
Alfie could hardly conceal his laughter at what his friend had just said, and just looked up and shook his head and mumbled, "No I've not seen anything but I'll ask the other boys and if they know anything I'll let you know."
And with that the two men thanked the boys and got back into their car and drove off down the road leaving the two boys in fits of laughter at the side of the road.
"You've done some dull things in your time boy but that tops it all," Big Jones told Alfie.

When Big Jones told Stumpy and DD about what had happened with the men in the suits Stumpy said to Alfie,
"I've always said that you're a wooden top, but now this goes to prove it".
"Aye," chipped in DD, "I always knew that you were as thick as a plank but I didn't think you were that thick."
"What do you mean?" said Alfie with a serious face as the other three boys were almost crying with laughter.
"What they are trying to say is that you must be as thick as one of them poles," said Big Jones who Alfie regarded as his best friend.
"And I thought that you were my mates, boys," said Alfie to the three hysterically laughing men.
"Don't worry pal we won't say a word," said Big Jones, but Alfie knew that as soon as they saw the rest of the boys that they wouldn't be able to resist telling them, and if he was honest he would do the same to them and they all knew that, and it took all of five minutes before everybody in the college knew about what had happened earlier in the day and as soon as Alfie set foot in the college dorm the dwarf shouted across to him.
"Hey, Alfie, is it true that you've put Busby out of a job?"
As the 4 days of the picket were coming to an end Alfie was glad to be going home to get away from all the jokes that were going about what he had done, and as he was on the minibus going back home he sat by his mate Big Jones.
"Don't forget now, boys, what went on up here stays up here."
But he knew that as soon as the boys got back home word would soon get around about what had happened to the telephone poles, and as Stumpy said to him, "There's more chance of you tossing one of them

poles in the highland games than there is of this lot keeping their mouths shut."
"Right enough, but I think he's the biggest tosser that I know so he might have a chance," said the dwarf taking another drag on his woodbine.
"Shut up, midget," snapped back Alfie, "and watch you don't fall off the end of that fag!"

The strike was fairly peaceful in the Welsh valleys. Although there were a few scuffles with the police it was generally good natured. Indeed a lot of the local police officers either had family or friends who worked in the mines and were mostly sympathetic to the miners' cause. The only real problems that occurred were when the police were joined by members of the army, which was denied at the time and is still denied to this day, although Alfie had a friend of his in the army who told him that all the soldiers in his battalion were asked who had family members or friends involved in the strike, and if they did they could opt out of picket line duties.

Chapter 9

One occasion that occurred was when word got out that there was to be an unofficial return to work at a colliery in the next valley and a picket line was to set up at the colliery gates.Big Jones and a selection of men were sent from the vale to join the men from the other collieries in the area in what was to be a peaceful picket to try and stop anybody from crossing the picket line who did not have the union's permission.
When the boy's got there, there was a large police presence and also a large amount of picketing miners. The police were backed up by officers on horseback: the first time that horses were used in Wales as far as the boys could tell, indeed nobody could think of any time that horses had been used before in this campaign. This was also the first time that the Welsh picket lines were infiltrated by outsiders who were there just to cause trouble, although they had seen this sort of thing on their trips into other areas outside of Wales and had heard stories, this was the first time that they had witnessed outsiders causing trouble.

One instance was when a young man with a close cropped haircut threw a stone at a police officer hitting him on the side of the head causing his helmet to fall off, and he vanished back into the crowd before he could be caught by the genuine miners who mostly wanted no trouble. This incident prompted the police to call for the police horses to be brought in, as the crowd by now was starting to gather .There was a lot of pushing and shoving from the back of the crowd and Big Jones found himself standing nose to nose with a youngster who did not look older than 19 or maybe 20 years of age in a police uniform, this officer had a helmet that was like a rubbish bin on his head and a uniform that was like a circus tent on him.

When he looked up at Big Jones you could see by the look on his face that he was scared and did not want to be there. Big Jones looked down at the boy and noticed that there was no number on the shoulder of his jacket where all police officers had their number. As the pushing got more and more severe the police horses were brought to the front of the crowd to try and control the pushing and once again there was interference from an unknown and unwelcome element of the crowd as a group of youngsters pushed their way forward to the front of the crowd where the police horses were gathered and one of them reached into his coat pocket and produced a tin of snuff which he blew into the horse's nostrils causing the horse to raise it self up on its hind legs crashing the front legs down almost landing on Alfie if it had not been for Lou to pull him back, but these yobs had not finished yet as with the horse by now sneezing violently and unable to see as well as he could due to its eyes watering due to the effect of the snuff another boy threw a handful of ball bearings under the horse's hooves, but this time he was not as lucky as his two mates, because as he threw the ball bearings the officer on the horse lashed out with his truncheon hitting the boy on the head sending a scattering of blood onto those who were near him.

As he tried to turn and run into the crowd he ran into the formidable figure of Leighton who was a very large man who spent his Saturday afternoons on the rugby field where he regularly destroyed men twice the size of this boy. Leighton was also an animal lover and as the boy looked at Leighton and tried to push past him Leighton let fly with a fist the size of a prize cabbage catching the boy in the mouth sending him crashing to the floor.

"That's for the horse!" Leighton growled at the boy.

"And this is for me," came a voice from behind Leighton that he did not recognise, as the unknown man sent a size nine boot crashing into the boy's side causing him to let out a loud gasp as you could hear the air escaping from his lungs. Leighton picked the boy up and dragged him to the front of the crowd where by now there was a large amount of police with truncheons drawn ready to lash out at anybody who stood in their way causing the crowd to quieten down. Leighton motioned for an officer to come to him, the officer must have seen the boy who Leighton had by the neck and went over to Leighton with

another officer and called him forward behind the police lines
"This is the one who threw the ball bearings at the horse," he said.
"And what happened to his face, did he fall down trying to run away?" asked the officer in a sarcastic tone.
"Yes," replied Leighton.
"I thought I saw him falling over, now leave him to us," said the policeman, as two officers dragged the boy away. Leighton watched them throw him into the back of a van to a round of clapping and cheering from the crowd.

By now word had got down to the picket line on the gate that there would not be anybody returning to work that day and everybody should return home as there was no more to be done there for now . Three days later Leighton's hand had swollen to twice its normal size and he went along to the local hospital where he was given an x-ray on his hand. When he was called back to see the doctor for the x-ray results he was asked by the doctor, "Have you been fighting?"
Leighton replied, "No, but why do you ask?"
"Well," replied the doctor, "how do you explain this?"
He pointed out to Leighton on the x-ray the remains of three teeth embedded in his hand.
Leighton tried to convince the doctor that they were old rugby injuries, but the doctor just gave him a look of disbelief and promptly booked him in to have a local anaesthetic to have the teeth removed, which he kept in a jar as a memento of the strike.

At weekend the boys were told that the committee at the local club had decided that the striking miners were to be given 25 beer checks a month for the duration off the strike, a decision that was more than welcome with the boys who were looking forward to spending their weekend in the house. Big Jones was first on the phone to Alfie and the two mates decided to go to the club that night to pick up their checks. As they went to the club that night they were both told by their wives that they had better keep some checks so that they could take them out the following week, and as they both knew if they didn't keep some back there would be trouble.

As they walked into the club they were told that there was a committee meeting going and that they would have to wait until the meeting was finished before they could get their checks.
"I bet Colin Asthma has had his checks, " said Alfie to Big Jones.
But they went into the bar and had a pint while they waited for the meeting to finish.
"Have you seen Stumpy?" Big Jones said to one of the regulars in the club.

"He came in this afternoon, but I don't know long he stopped," said the man.
"Must have got his checks and went home in case he had to buy somebody a pint," said Alfie with a sarcastic tone to his voice, and as he spoke Colin Asthma came into the bar and told the boys that the meeting had just finished and if they were quick they might catch Ade the club treasurer who was in charge of the checks. As the two boys ran up the stairs they could see Ade putting his coat on and they quickly went into his office to collect their checks.
"What you do two want?" said Ade.
"Our checks," said Big Jones.
"Too late tonight boys, come back tomorrow night," said Ade, who was not one of the nicest men when he wanted to get home.
"You'll have to come back tomorrow night," he repeated.
"What do you mean?" said Big Jones, stepping forward and slamming a fist the size of a bag of small coal into the filing cabinet which Ade had just put the beer checks into, causing the door of the cabinet to fall open to reveal bottles of spirits and cans of beer piled up inside, and as Big Jones and Alfie looked at the piles of drinks in the cabinet Ade reached in and grabbed a handful of checks and without counting them threw them on the table and told Big Jones and Alfie to get out of his office before he changed his mind about giving them their checks and make them wait until the following night, so the two boys just grabbed the checks and were down the stairs in a blue flash, laughing at what they had seen and overjoyed that at last they had got one over on Ade, who as Alfie would say was as ugly as a ten pound fine, and as mean as a cross-eyed tiger with toothache.

As they walked into the lounge of the club Colin Asthma was coming out and he asked the boys if they had been for their beer checks.
"Yes we had them just now, but we weren't offered a drink from the private cabinet," replied Alfie.
"What do you mean?" asked Colin with a bemused look on his face. But before Alfie could say any more he was almost lifted off his feet as Big Jones grabbed him by the arm and almost carried him into the lounge saying to Colin, "Don't take any notice of him, you know what he's like when he's had a drink" and with that they went through the door leaving Colin standing there wondering what that was all about. Half an hour later Stumpy came in and he had their mate Dan with him.Dan was blind but what he lacked in eyesight he made up for with a marvellous sense of humour and a witty remark for most occasions. This night it was particularly cold and the heating was on full, as the night went on Dan would ask if anybody was going to the toilet and somebody would normally take him.

This one night Dan asked if somebody would take him to the toilet, but before any one could answer Big Jones stood up and put a finger the size of a cigar by his mouth and shook his head and motioned for nobody to move, so as Dan was getting desperate to go the toilet nobody would take him until he sat there with his legs crossed and a look of desperation on his face, when Big Jones rose like a volcano out of his chair and said, "Come on Dan if they won't take you, can come with me," and as Dan got out of his seat Big Jones caught Dan by the arm and guided him to the toilet, but as he walked away he motioned to the rest of the boys to follow them. As Big Jones led Dan into the toilet he walked past the urinal and put Dan to stand against the radiator in the toilet which was on full, and as an unsuspecting Dan proceeded to relieve himself against the radiator the toilet began to fill up with steam, causing all who were there to laugh at what was happening with the exception of Dan who was blissfully unaware of what was happening, until he had finally finished and asked, "What are you lot laughing at?" but nobody said a word as they all tried to stifle their laughter amid a scene that resembled a Turkish sauna.

The night in the club finished as usual for Alfie with a stop in the fish and chip shop on the way home for his normal bag of pie and chips, but that night with all that had gone on Alfie had drunk more than he normally would and as he waited in the queue for his pie and chips he got talking to some of the other boys from the club and they chatted away waiting to be served. Alfie got served and walked out of the fish shop and proceeded to make his way home enjoying his supper when as he approached the house where Dan lived a terrible thought crossed his mind. He remembered that he had left Dan outside the fish shop. As Alfie hurriedly ran back up the street his mate Dan was still standing shivering where he had left him,
"Where you been," he said. "I'm freezing."
"Sorry Dan, the queue in there was crazy."
"Where's your food then? I can't smell anything."
"No," said Alfie, "by the time I got to the counter they had no pies left and I didn't want to keep you waiting too long so I didn't bother to have anything."
"Fair play to you," said Dan. So they made their way home with Dan unaware that Alfie had eaten his food as he walked half way home before he remembered about him.

The following morning Alfie woke with his normal Saturday morning hangover, which was a result of another night drinking with his good mate Big Jones.
"One day I'll see him off," said Alfie to his wife.
"You've been saying that for twenty years or more now, and I think

you'll be saying that in another twenty years," replied his wife.
"We'll see," said Alfie.
"Don't forget we are meeting Jonesy and his wife up the club tonight for a drink, or have you forgotten about that?" she said referring to the fact that Alfie would be going to watch his beloved rugby team that afternoon as he had done for as long as she had known him, as he would say every time he went, "A good shout at a referee on a Saturday afternoon relieves a lot of tension." It was a fact that his wife would back him up on, as when she went with him she was one of the most vocal spectators there.
"I know I'll be home in plenty of time to take you out," he promised.
"You are sure because I know what you're like when you go into the rugby club you lose all track of time, and if you don't come home I'll be up there looking for you!"

Alfie knew that she wasn't joking about coming into the club for him as she had done it before when he forgot that they were supposed to be going to a wedding about three years ago when she walked into the club with his suit and made him change in the toilet much to the amusement of all his friends there, and he made a promise to himself that he would never let that happen again as he was still getting it thrown up to him now, and the boys in the club still remind him of it from time to time. About 11o'clock Alfie went upstairs to the bathroom for a shave and a shower before going out for his normal Saturday fix of rugby.
"Right, I'll see you later, and before you start I'll be home by half past six."
"All right then but don't forget" she said as he kissed her on the cheek and made his way down the street to wait for his lift.

Alfie got home earlier than expected and his wife knew by the look on his face that his team had lost.
"Do you want anything to eat?" she said.
"No thanks, I've had a plate of curry and chips up the club before I came home," he mumbled: a thing she knew was a sure sign that his team had lost.
"What was the score then?" she asked.
"17-14 to them but we should have won if the ref was fair but he gave us nothing, and their second try came from a forward pass, but that's how it goes," he said with a look like a puppy on his face.
"Same story whenever they lose. I'll have to start coming with you again. They won the last few times I've been with you." But Alfie knew that although his wife loved to watch the rugby she understood that Saturday afternoon rugby was his way of letting off some steam.

That evening Alfie and his wife walked up to the club and as they went into the lounge Big Jones and his wife were sitting by the double door at the back of the lounge.
"Why are you sitting here?" asked Alfie.
But Big Jones just pointed to where they usually sat and said, "Look at all them down there; we are better off up here," and as Alfie looked to their normal seats there were a gang of women sitting there.
"I see what you mean, if we sat by them we wouldn't be able to get a word in, but they look like an ugly bunch, I wouldn't want a smack in the mouth off that one in the green dress."
"No she's got a fine pair of arms on her," remarked Big Jones.

As Big Jones went to get some drinks in Alfie went to the toilet, as he was in the toilet two of the women came in and stood next to him.
"Excuse me," he said with a look of surprise on his face, "but the ladies toilets are back down the corridor."
"We know that," replied a deep husky voice and as Alfie turned around he realised that the two women were indeed two men in dresses.
"Sorry, I thought you were women," said Alfie with a look on his face of horror.
"Don't worry about it mate it happens all the time," said the man who was now standing next to him.

Alfie hurriedly finished in the toilet and rushed back into the lounge where Big Jones was just sitting down with a round of drinks.
"Hey boy," he said, "Those women sitting in our seats are men in drag."
"What do you mean, men in drag, how much did you have to drink this afternoon?"
"I'm telling you two of them were in the toilet with me just now; they scared the life out of me."
Big Jones and the boys' wives looked down and they all agreed that they could now see that the women were indeed men.
"Never mind them," said Alfie's wife "as long as they keep to themselves they are not hurting anyone."
"Exactly," said Big Jones before anybody else could say anything, "Now just drink your beer and forget about them."
Alfie just sat down and mumbled, "Well I don't feel comfortable with them being here but as long as they stay down there I suppose it will be all right, but that one in the red dress reminds me of somebody."

As the two couples chatted away and were enjoying the night out the club started to fill up as it did on Saturdays, as Colin Asthma came in he looked at Alfie and asked him,"What was the score in the rugby to

day?"
"We lost 17-14, but we should have won," he replied, looking at Big Jones who normally tells them all to ask Alfie the score if they had lost, but he knew that Colin knew the score because if his team had won he would not have asked him, and his nephew played for the club, and it was the same thing with most of his mates in the club,if his side had won nobody mentioned the game but if they had lost,then they would all ask him.
"Anyway never mind about the rugby, what you lot on the committee going to do about that lot in dresses down there?" he asked Colin.
"Well they haven't done anything wrong and there are no laws against men wearing dresses so there's not much we can do about it," said Colin with a hint of a smile on his face.
"You won't be laughing if they start fetching their mates here and the locals stop using the club, then all your little committee perks will be finished."
"Don't talk soft they won't be coming here regular."
Alfie just grunted and said, "You wait till the next committee elections are on, me and Jones will put our names down, then there will be some changes here."

Colin just laughed and walked away without saying another word. As Alfie looked across at the men or she males as Big Jones was calling them by now the one in the red dress looked at him and smiled.
"Hey Jones the one in the red dress just smiled at me."
Big Jones looked over his shoulder and burst out laughing. "Well you did say that you thought you knew him. Are you sure it's not an old girlfriend?" That remark brought laughter from not only the two wives but also everybody in earshot of him. As Alfie looked back across, the man in the red dress rose from his seat and started to make his way over to where Alfie and Big Jones were sitting and he was smiling at them.
"Hey Jones he's coming over here, if he starts on me I'm going to smack him in the mouth."

But before Big Jones could reply the red dressed one was approaching the table and as he got closer Alfie got the feeling that he had seen this person before, but before he had the chance to think where a great big voice boomed out the words that gave it all away.
"What's the matter comrade?"
And Alfie realised to his horror that underneath the wig and behind the red dress and the make-up was his good friend Lou.
"What you doing dressed like that?" he muttered struggling to get his words out. As Lou sat down Alfie could feel his mouth going dry and his heart beating faster with the shock.

“Well,” said his mate, “I thought it was about time I came out and was honest about how I like to dress in women’s clothes, but I thought that you knew.”

Alfie struggled to get his words out: “How would I know?”
Lou laughed. “Well Big Jones has known for a long time.”
“Well he didn’t tell me, did you?” said Alfie looking at his other friend who was by now killing himself with laughter, as were their wives.
“Well I can’t see the funny side,” said a shocked Alfie. “Anyway how long have you been dressing like this?”
“About two years now, it all started on day when I put my wife’s dressing gown on by mistake one morning and it felt so soft that I decided to buy one for myself and one thing just led to another and now I’ve got a full wardrobe. The only things I don’t like are the high heeled shoes: they make my back bad after a bit, but I’ve got a nice pair of flat shoes on tonight.”

Alfie was stunned, but he was even more shocked at what Lou was to say next.
“Do you fancy trying on a dress, because if you do one of the boys with me tonight owns a dress shop and he can give you a good deal for first timers.”
Alfie looked at Big Jones that by now had tears rolling down his face. “Don’t laugh boy, you know what he’s like if you encourage him!” and as he turned to Lou he suddenly realised that all the men in dresses were now looking at him and laughing, as were the two wives, and it suddenly hit Alfie where he had seen the other two men in the toilet before. Lou was a member of the local Rotary Club and at the end of every month they used to dress up and go around the pubs and clubs in the area to raise money for charity and tonight was the end of the month.
“Got you comrade,” said Lou with a massive smile on his face as he slapped Alfie on the back as he normally did.

With that Lou walked away but he suddenly stopped and shouted back at Alfie and said, “I forgot to ask you but did your team win today?” and with that he sat back down on his chair.
“You all knew about this, didn’t you?” he asked but everybody around him were in fits of laughter and nobody answered him.
And as Lou and his mates were leaving the club they stopped by the table and shouted at him in unison
“Are you sure that you don’t want to come with us? ”

As the men went Big Jones told Alfie that when he went to the toilet

Lou came over and told everybody not to say anything to him because he was going to wind Alfie up as pay back for the time that he told the pigeon breeder that Lou also bred pigeons.
"Fair enough boy, but I'll have my own back, you'll see, and you lot can watch out too," he said looking at all his other mates who were in on the joke.

Chapter 10

On the Monday morning the boys were back up to Oxford to carry on with the campaign to fight for their jobs, needless to say Alfie was the main talking point on the way up with Big Jones and whoever else was in the club that night playing their part in the story. Oddball the driver was as usual late but as he pulled off he told the boys that he had found a farm not far from where the college was and he had asked the farmer if he could call in the next time he was passing.
"They sell all sorts of things there and I've been to see King Will and he's given me £20 out of the strike fund to buy some food."
"You must be a good one to get money off King Will," said Stump. "He's normally as tight as two coats of paint."
It was not too long before the minibus was driving down a bumpy lane to the farm.
"How did you find this place boy?" said Big Jones as he was shunted from side to side almost crushing Alfie who was sitting next to him pinned against the window.
"Took a wrong turn," came the answer. "Here we are," said Oddball. "I'll go and knock the door and see the farmer."

But Oddball was back in the bus sooner than he had planned as the farmer's dogs came running down the path from the farmhouse.
"Forgot about them," he panted as he dived back on to the minibus.
With that the farmer came out of the house to see what the dogs were barking at and as he spotted the minibus he called the dogs in to him and gestured for the minibus to follow him. As he walked down in front he stopped by a red brick building with two large wooden doors and as he opened the doors the boys could see some large kegs which looked like they were holding some sort of liquid.
"Come on and have a look to see what you want then," said the farmer who still had two of the dogs with him.
"What about the dogs?" asked Alfie?
"They won't hurt you as long as I'm here," said the farmer. As the boys stepped into the barn they were hit by a smell of rotten apples and it soon became clear that the kegs were cider vats.
"How much for the cider?" said Big Jones.
The farmer looked at him and rubbed his unshaved chin."I don't

know if I can sell you lot this stuff. The locals are only allowed to buy 2 pints at a time, and how do I know if you can handle my cider? There's been better men than you lot go down to my cider."
After much chit chat between the boys and the farmer he decided to sell them 2 gallons of cider but he would not put the cider into plastic bottles, but he told them that he would sell them 2 one gallon glass containers and if they came back again they could bring it with them and use it again, and he also let them have some home cured ham, butter and cheese for the £20 that Oddball had in his hand muttering to him, "You've just robbed me son."

But they all knew that it would take better men than them to catch a farmer. As the minibus pulled up outside the college Alfie was first off the bus with nothing but revenge on his mind but that would have to wait as there were more pressing things on the agenda for them.
"Right," said Jamie, "There's an open day at the fire station and they have said that we can take some buckets down there and make a collection for the striking miners, so if you grab a couple of buckets, Jock will be here in ten minutes to take you there."
"Come on boy," Big Jones said to Alfie. "Let's get down there; at least it's out in the open, and you know the firemen always give us tidy food, not like the muck in a truck that Lenny gives us here."
"Good thinking boy," replied Alfie. When they got to the fire station there was quite a crowd there and as the boys went in one of the firemen told them to go and get some food off one of the stalls and they would sort out some drinks for them, and somebody would make an announcement that some striking miners would be making a collection and all donations would be welcome.

The collection went better than expected as quite a lot of people put money into the buckets with a few people putting notes into the buckets. At the end of the afternoon the boys decided to carry on with the collection in the town centre as it was quite a nice day and took the short walk into town. When they got into the town they decided to go in separate directions and meet outside the labour club in an hour. The town was fairly busy and the collection had a mixed response from different people until the boys met up by the club where they spotted a woman sitting on the floor with her dress spread out around her and a piece of cardboard around her neck saying that she had no legs and had no money for food.
"Look at her," said DD, "and we think that we've got it hard, let's give her the money."

And as they emptied the money into her bowl they all felt that they had helped her out and felt pleased with what they had done. When they got back to the college Jamie asked them how it had gone and when they told him what they had done he felt proud of them. That evening they decided to try the cider as they did not have to go on picket duty until the following afternoon, so they got the cheese and ham and Alfie went to the shop for a loaf of bread and they seemed to be getting settled down for the night.

The cider was going down without a problem and the ham and cheese were very tasty and they could not see why the farmer was making such a fuss about selling it to them. As more of the cider was being consumed Big Jones looked over at Alfie and noticed that he was just staring into space and as he asked him if he was all right, he just looked at him and although his mouth opened no words came out.
"You've had enough boy, you're like a goldfish, your mouth is open but there's nothing coming out," he said, and he was not on his own as DD went to get up to go to the toilet he just fell straight towards Stumpy and as Stumpy tried to move out of the way he fell backwards and as he fell his legs came up and knocked the table over spilling the glasses and the container over the dwarf who tried to catch the glass jar but as he was seeing double he missed and as his hand went out he slapped Mansy in the eye.
"Right," said Big Jones, "I think we can leave it there for tonight, this cider is better than we thought."

Alfie again tried to talk but again no words came out and as he went to get up his legs would not move causing him to fall to the floor. Big Jones and the boys tried to pick Alfie up but the cider was starting to make its mark on all of them and Alfie was like a rag doll, falling back down every time they picked him up. He would go back down in a heap over and over again, so they decided to leave Alfie on the floor with a blanket over him for the night. The following morning the boys were woken by the boys who had been out on picket duty the night before and when Jock told them about the antics with the cider they made more noise than usual. Big Jones as usual was the first to wake and although he had consumed his share of the cider he looked as though he had not had a drink. Stumpy had his head under the blanket as he lay in a semi-coma on his cot mattress, until he heard the word cup of tea mentioned and he mumbled, "Two sugars in mine," as he lifted his head out of the blanket like a fish lifting its head out of the water catching flies.

Alfie was still lying down by the table with the blanket over him and it looked like he had not moved all night, but the one who looked the worst was Mansy. When he woke them they were all looking at him and asking him how he had got the black eye.

"What black eye?" he said as he went to the bathroom to look in the mirror. "How did I get this?" he asked but nobody answered as they could not remember much about the night before, but the black eye was soon forgotten as DD crawled out of his sleeping bag and looked down at Alfie and noticed that there was a patch on the carpet where the cider had spilled and as they looked around them there was a patch on the table where the varnish had been stripped off the table. "Look at that carpet and table," said DD "that's the last time I'll drink that cider!"

That morning as the boys were in the van going to the power station to do their duty on the picket line they were all feeling the effects of the cider from the night before and as Alfie and Stump jumped out of the van they decided that if it was quiet they would go in to the shed and try to get the effects of the night before out of their systems. After about an hour they had not seen any lorries trying to take coal into the power station so they decided to take turns to go into the shed and have a lie down. Stump was the first to go into the shed and Alfie said he would keep watch for any coal wagons trying to go into the power station.

Alfie sat down in the deck chair that had been given to them by one of the locals and it was not long before he heard the sound of snoring coming from the shed. It was quite a nice day and Alfie was happy to sit outside the shed, and soon he started to feel the effects of his hangover wearing off in the afternoon sun and soon he was dozing off himself. Alfie was suddenly woken up by the sound of voices and as he rubbed his eyes he could see two of the locals from the nearby village standing over him laughing and holding a basket and a flask. "We thought that you might like some coffee and sandwiches," they said putting the flask and basket on the floor by the side of his deck chair.

As Alfie opened the basket he took out a sandwich and poured some coffee and started to tuck in and was talking to two of the locals who were from the support group that had been formed for the striking miners and he forget about Stump sleeping in the shed when he heard a scream and as they all turned around they could see a cow with it's head in the shed and it was licking Stump's face.
"I thought that you were watching while I had five minutes," screamed a startled Stumpy.
"I was," Alfie replied laughing at his mate, "but when I saw the cow kissing you I thought that your luck might have been in, and you seemed to be enjoying yourself!"
"What you mean enjoying I? It scared the life out of me," said Stump

who by now was munching on a sandwich.
"Well I thought that you might have been dreaming about your wife and thought that she was kissing you," said Alfie trying to hide his laughter.

As Alfie and Stumpy sat outside the shed the two locals,who could see the funny side of things, made their way down the hill to where Big Jones and DD were.
"Don't tell the big boy and his Muppet friend about that cow, or there will be trouble," shouted Stumpy.

About an hour later Big Jones and DD came up the hill to where Stump and Alfie were and sat down on the floor by the side of Stump who by now had pinched the deck chair off Alfie.
"How's it been up here?" said Big Jones.
"Nothing happening," replied Alfie.
"Well we were told that you two were going to go early," said DD.
"What you mean going early? We can't go until the van comes for us," said Alfie.
"Why can't Stump's girlfriend ask the farmer to give you a lift?" replied Big Jones with a big grin on his face.
"What do mean you by that boy?" said Stump.
"Well the people who brought us sandwiches said that you had your tongue down some old cow's throat when they left you," came the reply from Big Jones.
"And what are you laughing at boy?" Stump snarled at DD.
"Nothing, I'm just glad that you've made a friend at last."
"Was it like kissing your wife?" asked Big Jones, but before Stump could answer DD passed him a sandwich which he had filled with grass.
"What's that for boy? I can't eat that," said an angry looking Stump.
"Well if it's good enough for your girlfriend then it should be good enough for you," he said as he ducked for cover as Stumpy threw the bread at him.
"And you can tell them two where they can stick their sandwiches, and tell them to keep out of my way."
"Well if you're not happy you can always get your girlfriend to give them a kick," said DD still with a big grin on his face.
"I'll kick you if you don't shut up," replied Stumpy, but he knew that this was not the last he had heard of this.

That night all was fairly quiet in the college with the normal amount of banter going on between the boys, until the boys who had been doing the afternoon picket duty came back in.
"How was it?" asked Alfie.

"Pretty quiet," replied Mansy who by now was sitting by Stumpy who had his usual mug of tea in his hand sitting on the baby's cot mattress he had found in a skip earlier.
"What do you want?" snarled Stumpy at the man he called the ugliest man in the world.
"Why do you think I want anything, I just want to sit by you because I like you," replied Mansy.
"Well I don't trust you Mansy, you remind of a bogey man, you're as ugly as a fifty pound fine, so just go and find a house to haunt, and what 's the smile on your face for?"
"Well," replied Mansy."You just can't be nice to some people," he said getting up and slapping him on the top of the head, which didn't do much for his mood. Just as Stumpy was getting up off the mattress to chase Mansy out of the room there came a clatter of feet coming up the stairs as the dwarf came into the room with a paper bag in his hand.
"What you got there boy?" asked Big Jones.
"Pie and chips so you can sit down or you'll eat the lot before I get the chance to eat anything."

As he sat down by the table he put the paper bag down on the table. He opened the bag and everybody looked at him in envy, with the smell of vinegar wafting around the room. The dwarf was soon getting stuck into his food not caring that all the eyes were on him when all of a sudden he stopped and looked and asked if anybody would like a chip, but before anybody answered he shouted across to Stumpy, "I would have bought you a pie but you might not have liked it."
"Why?" asked the silver fox.
"Well you know you might have been eating one of your girlfriend's families," he said just dodging the cup that Stump had launched at him.
"Who told you about that? Was it the big boy or his friend the Muppet DD?" snarled Stump.
"Nobody told me. It's on the front page of the Farmers' Times: man gets engaged to a cow."

The next few days were quiet and on the day they were due to go home they had a phone call to say that the minibus that was going to pick them up was going to be late so the boys decided to go into town and have a pint in the labour club. The walk into the town took about ten minutes and as it was quite a windy day they decided a brisk walk would do them all good. As they got to the town the woman who they had given the money was in the same spot and she gave them a smile and a wave.

"That's nice of her," said DD, "she didn't forget us."

But as the boys stopped to wave back to her a car drove past and with the force of the wind the woman's dress rose into the air and the boys could see that it wasn't that she had no legs, but she was standing down an open manhole with the cover hidden under her dress on the pavement.
"Look at that! She's down that manhole!" shouted the dwarf, "and we took pity on her and gave her our money."
But the woman just looked away and didn't seem to care as she simply rearranged her dress. When the boys got back to the college they were telling the students what they had seen in case they saw the woman and also gave her money, when the student who was sitting by Jamie on the day that they had told him what they had given the money to the woman for told them that she was well known in the area for conning people. "And you boys were the latest, and I don't think that you will be the last."

Chapter 11

With the winter fast approaching all the miners unions hopes seemed to be on stockpiles of coal at the power stations dwindling forcing power cuts which would help the miners cause for a settlement of the strike, but all the miners who had been on protests and picket line duties at various power stations up and down the country knew that this time the government had done their home-work and learned the lessons from the 72 and 74 strikes and that there was plenty of fuel stockpiled to ensure that there would be no power cuts. The same thing could not be said for the striking miners as all concessionary coal was stopped partly due to the Coal Board, but more importantly the coal wagons from the colliery coal yards were only delivering to pensioners and schools. The colliery where the boys worked had a man returned to work and it was decided to put a picket outside the colliery gates, needless to say the police presence was quite formidable and nobody was allowed to take cars past the square which was a mile and a half from the colliery, so as the police decided to turn the cars back; the only option was to park the cars and walk to the colliery. Despite the police making things difficult there was still a good turnout at the gates of the colliery and when the police van with the scab as he was known came there was a rush from the picketers and also some of the local people who gave their support, but the van just drove past totally ignoring the protests of the people on the road.

Some of the police were sympathetic to the miners, indeed some of the police had families and friends who were past and present miners, but as they would say they were only doing as they were told otherwise their jobs would be at risk. As time went on the lone returnee as the Coal Board would call him or the scab as he was more widely called was joined by four more, and this resulted in more tension between the police and the picketers on the gate especially when the police decided to put a limit of no more than 4 men to stand on each gate. The fact that a hundred men or more would gather at the gates meant that this was only going to cause more trouble between the miners and the police which amounted to a few scuffles when the men tried to push forward when the van arrived and inevitably there were a few arrests made.

It was on one of these cold dark December mornings that one of the saddest events of the strike occurred in the Welsh valleys. A police car arrived at the gates and as King Will was spotted in the back seat it was widely thought that he must have been arrested, but as the car stopped and King Will stepped out it was clear for all to see from the expression on his face that there was something wrong. As King Will moved amongst the men they were all asking him what was wrong but King Will just moved silently forward until he reached the gate and stepped up on to the small wall.
"Comrades," he said speaking in a very emotional tone, to a now hushed crowd, "I have some sad news for you; this morning there was a taxi bringing a man to work at this colliery."
He stopped to catch his breath and seemed to wipe a tear from his eye. "There was an unfortunate incident where a concrete block was dropped off a bridge and went through the windscreen killing the taxi driver."
The crowd were by now shocked and sickened, this was not what they wanted. This strike was about saving jobs not about taking innocent lives. King Will carried on with his speech; his voice by now was trembling with emotion. "Boys go home there's nothing to be done here today. Let's all go home and let our thoughts be with the family of this poor man especially at this time of year, who was only doing his job whatever people may think and has paid a terrible price for it."

Nobody said a word as they all silently walked away past the line of police officers who were standing silently watching as the miners made their way home, heads bowed and with tears in their eyes. The next few days were spent away from the picket line at the colliery due to respect for the taxi driver and a lot of people were questioning what the strike was achieving and if it was now time to call off the strike, but when it was looked at the other side of things the industrial action was not about money but saving jobs and however sad it was about what had happened the strike had to be carried on.

Chapter 12

As the strike started to eat into the months there was still a lot of support from people outside the mining industry and people started to donate food to the unions, with some food being donated from as far as Eastern Europe. The food was divided into parcels and was shared out equally among the striking miners. A transit van was donated by a local garage and was driven by Dai Rugby, although some one said that it looked like the van was going by itself as Dai couldn't see over the steering wheel. Everybody was grateful for the food parcels even though some complained that all they were getting was corn beef and mincemeat and someone remarked that if you hadn't cut your finger on a tin then you were not a striking miner; but at the end of the day beggars can't be choosers and they were mostly very grateful.

One day King Will was approached outside his office,(which was commonly known as the shed) and was asked when the food parcels were going to be shared out. King Will looked at the man in amazement and explained that the food parcels were being distributed on a regular basis, when the man said that there were five miners living in the street behind him who had all had food parcels on three occasions but that he had not had any. King Will was shocked and told the man that he would find out for him and asked the man for his address, as luck had it Jamie and Dai Rugby and a few other boys pulled into the yard to load the van with food parcels when King Will stopped them to tell them what the man had said about not getting any food parcels. It was only then that it was discovered that they were taking the food parcels to the wrong address. Instead of delivering to number 96 they were delivering to number 69, who were accepting the food parcels and saying nothing.

Generally though people in the valleys were honest and trustworthy, but as you will find anywhere you do get the odd few who will try and make something out of other people's misery, such as the time when some of the boys were out in the town handing out leaflets asking for people to help support the strike and if they could donate a tin of food for the food hampers when a woman approached Alfie and told him that although her father was a retired miner and she had a lot of sympathy for what the miners were fighting for she thought that it was wrong that they were asking for donations for food parcels when over the other side of town in the car park there was a group of people with buckets asking for donations for the strike fund. As soon as Alfie heard this he went to find Jamie who was in charge of the collection to ask him why there was another group of miners on the other side of town and people were starting to complain.

Jamie told Alfie that as far as he knew there was nobody else out collecting and he would find out what was happening. As he was talking to Alfie, Big Jones, and DD came on to the scene and before Jamie could say anything they were off like a shot to find out what was happening. Big Jones and DD ran across the bridge in the centre of the town which was the quickest way to the car park followed closely by Alfie and Jamie who was shouting to Big Jones: "Keep a cool head and don't do nothing daft." There was a group of youngsters aged from about 16 to 20 years of age walking around the car park with buckets covered with paper that claimed to be from the local colliery, as Big Jones and DD saw these youngsters they stopped running and stood and watched what was happening from a distance, which gave Alfie and Jamie a chance to catch up with them, for them all to get a chance to get their second wind.

As the four men looked on in silence DD was the first to speak "Let's go down there and rip their heads off," he said in his usual delicate tone.
"Hang on punchy" retorted Jamie, "before you go and rip anybody's head off let's go and see what's happening they might be from another area, so let's find out first what they've got to say."
So the men decided to walk over and ask these youngsters what was happening and where they were from. Jamie led the way with DD and Big Jones behind him and Alfie was a few yards behind them. As they got closer to the youngsters it became clear that they were not known to any of the boys and it seemed that they were not taking any notice of the four men approaching them.
"How's it going boys?" said Jamie as he came within touching distance of one of the bucket collectors.
"Not bad" replied the boy,
"What you collecting for then, anything good?" asked Jamie, who could see Big Jones almost snorting down his neck.
"We're collecting for the miners. Do you want to donate any money?"
"What pit lodge are you collecting for then?" replied Jamie.
"That one down the road," replied the boy who by now had one of his mates by him who was looking a bit uneasy as he looked at the size of the two men standing behind Jamie.
"Do you mean the ale?" asked Jamie,
"Yes," replied the boy who by now looked like he was sensing that there was something wrong as DD was moving behind him.
"Well we all work in the vale pit and we don't seem to know you boys, so how are you collecting money for something that doesn't

concern you?"

Jamie's shoulder catching hold of the boy and all that Jamie could see was Before the boy could answer a hand the size of a football reached over the boy being lifted off his feet and Big Jones had him in his grasp which was like a vice.
"We were only trying to make some money. We didn't mean to hurt anybody," said the boy who was now almost in tears.
As Jamie turned around he could that DD had caught hold of the second boy while the rest of them had dropped their buckets and had run like the wind over the bridge.
"You can have the bucket," the second boy was saying to DD who was threatening to throw him off the bridge into the water. As he looked over Big Jones had the other boy upside down and was shaking all the money out of his pockets.
"Let them go boys," said Jamie, "before somebody calls the police. We can take the buckets and put the money into our strike fund."
So with a crowd of people now starting to gather around to see what was happening, Jamie explained what was happening and the two boys were now making a hasty retreat out of the car park with the crowd of people who had gathered cheering for what the miners had done to these boys who were trying con people.

As Christmas approached there was not a great deal of Christmas cheer being felt by the boys, who normally by now would be looking forward to the Christmas festivities Stumpy as normal had a plan, he and his mate Ade would be going out to get some Christmas trees from the forestry commission and sell them cheaper than the shops.
"How are you going to do that boy?" asked Big Jones. "The forestry people are not going to give you anything."
"Not going to ask them," he replied. "Ade used to work there and we are going to go up there with his van early Sunday morning before the forestry workers start their shift. He knows where the fence is down and they don't start work until 10 o'clock on a Sunday so we'll be up there by 5 o'clock and be gone before they start work."
Big Jones had a wicked grin on his face as he looked at Stumpy.
"What you grinning at?" Stumpy asked him.
"Well remember the last time you had a job to do for Ade?" he asked Stumpy, "when he offered you 10 pounds to paper the lounge in the club, and after you had finished we found out that he had been paid 30 pounds so he had 20 pounds for doing nothing except knocking your door, but good luck boy if you want to be stupid again. I know I wouldn't trust him: I'd rather trust a one-eyed snake than Ade," said Big Jones," and how many trees are you going to cut down in 3 hours?"

"We'll get a few and if they sell we will go back next week and get some more," replied Stumpy with a grin on his face," and I haven't forgotten about the papering but I'll have him back for that again and don't you say nothing to the rest of the boys especially DD, and thank you for those few kind words."

Chapter 13

Sunday morning arrived and Ade was there for Stumpy at 4-30 in the morning to go up to the forestry,
"What you got in the bag?" Ade asked Stumpy as he got into the van.
"A flask of tea," came the reply.
"It will be cold up there and we'll need something to warm us up."
"We'll have no time for tea; we'll be in there and gone in no time," said Ade. When they got to the forestry, Ade parked his van by the fence and sure enough it still had not been fixed so he drove the van in with the lights off so as no one would see to be on the safe side.
"I thought you said that they don't start work until 10," said Stump.
"I know," said Ade, "but we have got to be careful just in case. Sometimes the forest warden comes in early to look for people trying to steal trees."
"Well there are some dishonest people about so you can't blame him." Ade looked at Stumpy with one of his grumpy expressions and said, "Don't forget that this is part of the national park so if we do get caught it could mean a jail sentence and the van being confiscated. This is serious stuff so don't forget be careful and if you do see anybody just shout and we'll get out of here as quick as we can."

Stumpy understood what Ade was saying but his wicked side took over as he said to Ade, "I'll be watching like a little sniper and if I see anybody all you'll see is a blue flash and a smell of burning rubber as I clear those trees." But Ade as usual didn't see the funny side. Stumpy got out of the van and opened the back door to find a brand new bow saw, a shovel and a pair of gloves. "Is this all the tools you've got?" he asked Ade.
"Yes" replied Ade. "I only carry what I need, and it will give us more room to put trees in the back, so just get on with it and stop moaning, because the quicker the trees are chopped down and put in the van the quicker we can get out of here."
"Well if you had two saws we could both work at the same time," said Stumpy.
"Yes, and if we were both working at the same time we might not notice if somebody comes to work early and catches us; so just keep

your eyes open while I make a start."

Stumpy sat down on the log which was lying nearby and was keeping a watch as Ade had asked him to do. As Ade started busily sawing away at a tree he heard the striking of a match and as he looked over his shoulder he saw Stumpy lighting up a cigarette the glow of it.
"What are you doing?" he screamed at Stumpy, "if there is anybody here they will see the glow of the cigarette and they will be down here in no time. Do you want us arrested for trespassing and stealing from the forestry?"
Stumpy looked up at Ade and burst out laughing.
"What you laughing at?" he said through clenched teeth.
"Well," replied Stumpy, "you remind me of a garden gnome with that hat you've got on."
"Never mind the hat, just concentrate on why we are here."

What Stumpy did not tell Ade was he was laughing because Ade had a stammer and when he got excited or angry he could not get his words out,he had a habit of hitting his leg, and he was thinking about the time that he was calling bingo on the stage in the club when he couldn't get his words out, and in his frustration he couldn't hit his leg as he was sitting down with his legs under the stand which the bingo machine was on and so instead he hit the stand but in his frustration he hit the stand too hard causing the bingo machine to fall off the stand and landed on the stage floor smashing the bingo machine to pieces and sending bingo balls flying into the crowd.

As the time passed they had sawn down 5 trees and Stumpy decided to have a cup of tea.
"OK," said Ade, "but keep your eyes open." Stumpy sat down and poured some tea into his cup from the flask and as he sat down he started to doze off to sleep when he suddenly heard Ade shouting: "T, t,t,t,timber!" and as the word 'timber' came out of his mouth the tree landed on Stumpy, causing Ade to shout, "Too late!"
Stump's tea landed down his legs and he was covered in pine and branches from the tree leaving him with scratches to his neck and face and a cut to his mouth.
"You did that on purpose!" he screamed at Ade as he scrambled out from under the tree.
"Don't be daft" said Ade, " if I had done it on purpose I would have picked a bigger tree than that one, but anyway it could have been worse," said Ade who by now was having trouble getting his words out through the stammer and laughter at the sight of Stumpy under the tree.

“What do you mean worse? If it had been any worse I might have broken my neck,” said Stumpy resisting the urge to punch Ade in the mouth.
“Well it could have broken your flask or it could have been me” came the reply.

Monday night came and as usual the boys met in the club and were given 25 beer checks each by the committee as it was the first Monday of the month. Big Jones, Alfie and DD were the first to arrive and they collected their checks and made their way to the lounge to have a pint, and as they were walking down the stairs Ade was walking up to go to the committee room to do his normal duties as club treasurer.
“Where’s Stumpy then?” he asked in his usual sarcastic voice.
“Why boy?” retorted Big Jones in a tone that made Ade understand that he did not like him.
“Well you haven’t heard, have you?”
“Heard what?” interrupted Alfie, and Ade went on to tell them about what happened in the forestry the previous morning.
“Come on let’s have a pint and wait for the silver fox,” said DD. “This is something I’m not going to miss,” he added, thinking about all the tricks Stumpy had pulled on him.

Colin Asthma was next to come in. As he sat down he asked the boys had they heard about Stumpy.
“Yes Ade told us. How did you find out?”
“ I heard this morning in the shop,” he said.
Just then Stumpy came into the club and he went straight up the stairs to get his checks.
“Stand by the toilet boy,” Big Jones said to Alfie. “Then tell him that I want him in the lounge.”

Sure enough Stumpy came down the stairs and as he spotted Alfie standing by the toilet door he turned to go back up the stairs
“Where are you going?” Alfie shouted after him
“Be there now,” he said without lifting his head up.
“Well don’t be long. We want to see you in the lounge.”
Stumpy came back down the stairs and as he looked up Alfie could see that he had a black eye and cuts and bruises to his face, neck and lips and it was all he could do to stop himself from laughing. As he went into the lounge DD, Colin Asthma and Big Jones all looked at him and burst out laughing.
“How did you do that boy?” asked the big fella.
“Done it in the garden today,” he replied.
“How did it go yesterday then?” asked DD before anybody could say

another word.
"What do you mean? I was in the house all day," he replied in a quiet voice which he always did when he had something to hide.
"Well we heard that you were down in the woods with Goldilocks and you got attacked by the special branch," said DD not being able to wait to have a go at the man who had taunted him so much in the past few months.

By now all the boys were laughing and Stumpy was sitting there and telling Big Jones that he would never tell him anything again.
"It wasn't me; you had better go and see Ade; he's the one who told them, not me."
"I will as soon as he comes out of that committee meeting; I'll give him a flying head butt to the knee caps," said Stumpy referring to the fact that Ade was over six foot tall and Stump only five foot three or as Big Jones called him too short to go to a long dance.
Colin Asthma got up off his chair to go to the bar for a round of drinks and as he walked past Stumpy he said to him, "Good on you Stump, it's about time somebody chopped him down to size," causing Stumpy's face to turn red in anger as everybody started to laugh.

As Christmas drew closer, the club decided that this year all the striking miners who were members of the club would be invited to the old age Christmas dinner. A list was to be put on the notice board and all who wanted to go were to put their names on the list and specify if they would like a turkey or chicken dinner or a T-bone steak, as the food would be brought in by a catering company. Stumpy and Lou were the first to put their names down followed by the rest of the boys and in all there were eleven striking miners who wanted to go.
"Are we going to have any free beer?" Alfie asked Colin Asthma.
"I don't know but..." Before he could finish his sentence Lou interrupted him.
"You must be joking, free beer? The committee will be having that for their Christmas party after they kick us out."
"Well what more do you want? You are having a free meal plus the club is going to put on a singer later as well," replied Colin taking a puff on his inhaler as he usually did when he was annoyed or angry.
Lou just looked at Colin and just him and started to mimic the motions of somebody reeling a fish in out of the water saying, "You bite every time, if you were a fish you would jump straight into the pan."
"How would he know what a fish does? He's never seen one," said Stumpy referring to the fact that Colin was a keen fisherman.

The food finally arrived and everybody sat down in the hall looking forward to a night on the club.Stumpy made a remark that Big Jones should have his food first because if he was left to wait any longer he might start to chew somebody's arm off as he had told him earlier that he was so hungry that he could eat a photo of the last supper. The meal started with soup and a bread roll which was followed by the main course. While most people chose either chicken or turkey, Stumpy, Alfie and Lou chose to have steak, with Lou and Alfie opting for sirloin and Stumpy choosing a T-bone steak.

All was fine with the soup and everybody seemed happy with their meals except Stumpy, he thought that his T-bone steak was all bone and no meat. As the waitress came to his table to see what the problem was, Stumpy told her that he was not happy with the steak he was given and could it be changed.The waitress looked at the steak and in a somewhat sharp tone of voice told Stumpy that as he had ordered a T-bone steak that was the only one that was available so he had to eat what he was given.

Stumpy was not very happy with what he was told and said to the waitress, "Do you think I'm a dog because that is all this steak is fit for?"

But she just walked away saying she can do nothing: "There is nothing else available as I have told you."

Stumpy was not happy and shouted after the waitress, causing most of the people to look to see what was happening.

"Well if you're going to treat me like a dog, I might as well act like one!" and he promptly put his plate on the floor and got down on his hands and knees and started to bark like some sort of demented poodle, causing most of the people to stop eating and turn to watch what was happening. The waitress came running over and asked him what he was doing.

"Well," said Stumpy who by now had a crowd of people looking over at him most of whom were laughing, as well as Big Jones and the rest of the boys who by now were in tears of laughter. " I told you that if you want to treat me like a dog I might as well act like a dog."

The furious waitress was just about to pick up the plate off the floor when a man appeared and explained that he was the manager of the catering company and told the waitress to go and serve somebody else and he would deal with the situation, as by now people were standing on the tables and chairs to get a better view. The manager was a man of around 45 and he was smartly dressed in a suit and spoke in a slight Irish accent and he politely asked Stumpy if he would sit back on his seat so that the rest of the people could carry on with their meals and he would listen to his complaint.

Stumpy sat back down on his chair and put the plate back on the table and the manager agreed that it was not the best T-bone steak that he had seen and removed the plate saying that he would see if he could get him another meal to replace it, and he also said that the waitress that served him was new to the job and that he could only apologise to him, and with that he turned on his heels to go and sort out a meal for him. Big Jones looked across at Stumpy but before he could say anything he snarled at the big fella.
"Don't say a word or you'll be eating that turkey through a straw," and as Colin Asthma went to say something he interrupted him before he started saying it.
"And if you open your mouth you will have your next meal in a hospital bed, because I blame you for this."
"Why me?" asked Colin.
"Well if you and your committee mates had got tidy caterers in the beginning none of this would have happened."
Just as Stumpy was starting to let Colin know what he thought of the committee, the catering manager turned up with a turkey dinner for him.
"What's that?" he asked.
"A turkey for dinner you," came the reply. Stumpy looked at the plate of food and with a hint of a smile looked at him and said, "I didn't want a turkey dinner but I'm so hungry I don't care, so just put it down and thank you." Before anybody could say another word he started to devour the food. When everybody had finished their meal Stumpy was still munching away, so when the waitress asked about desert he told her that he didn't want anything but he would like a cup of coffee. When she returned with the coffee, Alfie looked at the cup and nudged Big Jones saying quietly, "He won't be happy with that cup, it's too small!"
Sure enough as soon as Stumpy saw the cup which was a proper coffee cup, he said to the girl, "I didn't order an eye wash," and he started to pick the cup up to his eye, but before he could go any further the girl took the cup off him and quickly went for a mug, to avoid another fiasco.

Chapter 14

As Christmas Eve arrived the boys were planning their usual night in the club which was holding the usual Christmas amateur talent show for the members, with a prize of £20 for the winner and £5 for the runners up. Stumpy as usual had his name on the list to sing along with most of the boys. Alfie and Big Jones were both told by their

wives that they would be coming up later so they had better keep them seats.
"And I don't want to be sitting by Stumpy this year," said Alfie's wife. "Last year I was sitting on his deaf side and I shouted so much that I lost my voice and I couldn't talk for days after."

Alfie just laughed and thought to himself that maybe it would be a good thing to leave her sitting there again, but he did not say it aloud because he knew that she had the money and he was not going to upset her. As Alfie and Big Jones walked up to the club Alfie told Big Jones that he had had a letter that morning about when he went for a medical examination about the scar he had on his nose due to an accident he had at work.
"Was there post today boy?" enquired the big fella.
"Must have been unless Santa dropped an early Christmas present through my letter box. They told me I have been awarded £190."
"Have you told the boss?" said Big Jones with a big grin on his face, referring to Alfie's wife as he always called her.
"Of course I have and if I didn't you would and then there would be trouble."
Big Jones just laughed and didn't answer as he knew that Alfie was right, but he couldn't resist saying, "Well I think that you are lucky to get that much."
Alfie looked at the big fella.
"Why?" he asked, "I broke my nose as well as this scar so I think I should have had more than that, and if we were working as normal I would turn it down but it is handy now that we are still on strike."

But Big Jones as always had the last word: "What I mean is you look better with the broken nose; it is an improvement and if the Coal Board could see you they might ask you to give them £190 instead."
Alfie knew that he would never get the last word so he kept his mouth shut and carried on walking to the club; as they walked into the club Alfie said to Big Jones, "Don't tell this lot in here about the money. You know what they are like. They will all want a pint and I haven't had anything yet."
"Don't worry boy; I won't say a word " and Alfie knew that although Big Jones was wicked he was a good friend and he could keep a secret when he wanted to.
"Come on then boy give me your coat and you can go and get the beer in as you are a rich man."
"Shut up Jones they might hear you," said Alfie as he looked across the room to see who was there. Alfie went to the bar and Big Jones went over to where they normally sat and put his and Alfie's coat over two chairs so that they would be kept for their wives. As he came

back to his seat Colin Asthma came over and sat down and he wasn't looking too happy.
"What's wrong boy? You look like you've been sacked off the committee," asked Big Jones.

Colin looked at him and said, "Well you know how much my wife loves her cat?"

"I know; she thinks more of the cat than she does of you," said Alfie with a grin on his face.

Colin continued "I went fishing this morning before she went to work and when I came home I found the cat dead in the lane behind the house. It looked like it had been hit by a car, so I picked it up and quickly buried it in the garden behind the shed, as my wife never goes up there as it full of my fishing stuff, before she came home from work."

"Did she find it then?" asked Big Jones, who by now was eager to find out what happened next.

"No, she came in and had a cup of tea and I thought I would not say nothing and let her think that the cat was out. When she finished her tea she went upstairs to take her work clothes off and I thought that she was upstairs a long time, so I went up thinking that she had fell asleep on the bed. As I was walking up the stairs I could hear her talking to someone and as I went into the bedroom she was lying on the bed and the cat was next to her: I had only gone and buried someone else's cat not ours"

Alfie and Big Jones could not contain their laughter as Colin looked so sorry for himself.

"Never mind," said Alfie, "there's a good show on tonight so it will take your mind off things."

"What's here then?" said Colin. "I didn't look at the notice board when I came in."

"Cats" said Alfie with a wicked grin on his face as Big Jones was killing himself laughing at Colin's expression.

"What have you bought your wife for Christmas?" Colin asked Alfie trying to change the subject.

"A chair," replied Alfie, "but I can't get a plug to fit it." But Colin was not in the mood for laughing even though Big Jones was chuckling, not at what Alfie had said but at Colin's pitiful expression.

The night went on and Colin was still not too pleased as word got round about the cat and numerous wise cracks were made. Alfie and Big Jones's wives came into the hall and sat down by the boys who were also joined by DD and Stumpy.

"What's wrong with Colin, is he all right?" asked Alfie's wife.

Before Alfie could say a word Big Jones quipped, "The cat's got his tongue," and Alfie, DD and Stumpy were in fits of laughter, with the two wives sitting there wondering what was going on. The evening carried on in the same manner and before long the talent show started. Colin Asthma was first on to the stage to sing and he set the marker for the rest of the contestants but as usual at the end of the night Stumpy was in the final, but it was not to be his night as he finished third and did not get a share of the prize money.

Alfie went to the toilet and as he was standing there he looked down and he spotted a twenty pound note by his feet, looking around to see if an body else had seen it he stepped back and bent down as if to tie his shoe laces and picked the money up and put it into his pocket and got out of the toilet as quick as he could and back into the hall.
"Drink up," Alfie said to big Jones," I've just found twenty pounds in the toilet, so we'll have a free night."
The night went on and Alfie and Big Jones spent the money that Alfie had found, but they did not tell their wives about the money Alfie found, because they did not try to find out who the money belonged to.
The following morning Alfie was nursing a massive hangover but he tried not to show his wife as he helped to prepare the Christmas dinner.
It was only when his wife asked him if he had spent the twenty pounds that she had given him the previous afternoon, that Alfie had a terrible flashback to the night before, and the money that he had found in the toilet was not money that somebody else had dropped, but money that he had dropped out of his own pocket, but he decided he was not going to say anything to anybody else because he knew that it was better not to say anything as he would never hear the end of it, so he told his wife that he had spent the money.

Chapter 15

With Christmas and the new year over, the talk was once again of how long the strike would last. It was reported in the media that there was to be a meeting with the N.C.B but no details were known as yet. The New Year started with the sad loss of an old colleague of the boys who died after a long illness, and on the 3rd of January they all attended his funeral, or as Big Jones would call it a planting. As usual for a funeral they all met in the club for a pint before the funeral and then made the short journey to the cemetery in the bus which was provided by the club, which they did for all deceased members. It was a cold wet day as the boys stood by the grave-side to pay their last respects.

Big Jones looked around and said quietly to Alfie, "There's not many here, I thought old George would have had a better send off than this." Alfie just nodded in agreement as the trumpeter was about to play the last post, as old George was an ex-soldier. As the last post sounded Alfie started to laugh.
"What are you laughing at boy?" said Big Jones as he looked at Alfie in amazement, but as he did he could see Stumpy pointing and saying: "Look at that!" and as he looked up he could see around a hundred men coming over the hill from the other side of the cemetery, realising when they heard the last post playing that they were in the wrong funeral, causing a lot of people to raise a smile, and as Stumpy said, "They were coming over the hill like commando's, George would have liked that." As the funeral party returned to the club for the reception the talk was of other funerals that they had attended, not in a morbid way but in a way of paying tributes to lost friends and colleagues. They eventually came around to the night that their colleague Bunion had collapsed and died by the bus stop while waiting for the bus to take them to do a night shift.

The man was known as Bunion by everybody and nobody can ever recall him being called by a Christian name, in fact nobody knows if anybody working with him knew his real name. The night he died Big Jones, Alfie and Lou were standing by him, and DD was in the nearby shop buying a pie as he had forgotten his food box. As Bunion collapsed Big Jones was first to try to give him mouth to mouth resuscitation as he was a trained first aider, but it was clear that Bunion was dead before he hit the floor.
"Phone for an ambulance", shouted Alfie, and as Lou was about to run to the club to use the phone Big Jones caught him by the arm and said, "Don't do nothing boy, if the coal board find out he died by the bus stop his wife will not get anything." Lou and Alfie looked at Big Jones in shock. Big Jones continued, "If they find out where he died they will not give her his coal and his pension."
"So what do we do then?" asked Alfie who was shaken with shock.
"Well we will wait for the bus and when it comes we will carry him on to the bus and take him with us to the colliery."

As DD came out of the shop he saw Bunion being picked up off the floor, and before he could say anything Big Jones motioned for him to be quiet as the bus was approaching. When the bus stopped Big Jones told Alfie to get on first and try to stand in front of the driver while he carried Bunion on the bus with Lou and DD. When they got him on the bus they were lucky that they were the first to be picked up and the bus was empty so they moved to the back of the bus. Not many more got on the bus and nobody seemed to notice that Big Jones was supporting Bunion who he had put on the inside of him.

The bus pulled up outside the colliery and Alfie got off and told the driver that he thought that he had a flat tyre on the back of the bus, causing the driver to get off the bus to have a look giving Big Jones and Lou time to get bunion off the bus and through the colliery gates where they carried on walking until they came outside the canteen where they put him on the floor.Big Jones then ran into the colliery baths where the medical centre was located and ran in and asked if there was a nurse on duty and told her to come quick as somebody had collapsed outside the canteen. The nurse quickly ran to the canteen where by now a crowd had gathered but she checked Bunion's pulse and said she thought he was dead and called an ambulance to take him to the local hospital where it was confirmed that he had died. It was a sad night but in the end it turned out that it was the right thing to do as his wife did manage to claim the coal allowance and the widow's pension.

As they carried reminiscing about friends that they had lost Stumpy made a comment.
"When I go I hope all of you lot will give me a send-off like old George had"
Quick as a flash big Jones chipped in
"Well I hope that you don't want to be cremated"
"Why" snapped the white haired one
"Well with the amount of alcohol you have drunk over the years, the flames will go on for 3 weeks boy"

So it was back to Oxford and the picketing duties: all hopeful that the strike would end soon. The first day back in Smith House was almost like starting out again but the boys soon got back into the swing of things. That night one of the students came into the students' bar carrying a box and asked if anybody knew anything about birds as he had found an owl and nobody knew what to do. Alfie told the student that he had seen an R.S.P.C.A. office in the town and he would take it down there in the morning. Big Jones looked at Alfie and said through gritted teeth, "Why did you say that? Where can we keep an owl until the morning?" But he knew that it was not worth talking to Alfie when he had had a drink so they just took the box that the bird was in and went back to the house. When they got back some of the boys except the Dwarf, were sleeping and some were still down the pub in the town.
"Where are they all boys?" asked Big Jones.
The Dwarf looked at the box and enquired what was in it and Alfie told him to mind his own businessman. Alfie put the box down by the

side of him.
“Where’s Stumpy then?” he asked.
“Gone up to the top room to have a sleep with Morgan. They said it is too noisy in here and they are on the picket line in the morning,” replied the dwarf still trying to look into the box. As the rest of the boys came in they all asked Alfie what was in the box and he told them the story about the owl and that he was going to take it down to the R.S.P.C.A. in the morning.

With that Colin Asthma asked to have a look at the owl saying that his brother used to have a pet owl and he knew a little bit about them, as Alfie opened the box for Colin to look inside the owl flew out of the box and up the stairs to the top room where Stumpy and Morgan were fast asleep.
“What are we going to do now?” Alfie shouted to his asthmatic friend.
“Well we have got to catch it,” wheezed Colin as everybody else laughed.
“Who do you think I am, Peter Pan?” asked Alfie as he ran up the stairs after the bird.
When they got up to the top room the owl had perched on top of the wardrobe in the corner of the room and Alfie and Colin decided top leave the bird where it was until the morning and then they would to try to catch it, so they went back down the stairs to join the rest of the boys and told them that the bird was safe for the night, and after a while they were all fast asleep.

Around 3.0 o‘clock in the morning they were all awoken by the sound of screaming from upstairs and Morgan running down the stairs followed closely by Stumpy with just their underpants on.
“What’s up with you two?” Big Jones said as he jumped up to see what all the fuss was about.
“There’s a ghost up there” said Morgan as he was standing there trembling with cold and fright.
“Yes,” said Stumpy trying to hide the fact that he too was scared.
By now they were all awake and looking at Morgan and Stumpy and shouting at them to go back to the top room.
“I’m not going back up there,” they said together.
“The place is haunted!” shouted Stumpy as the rest of the boys were all by now laughing at him.
“Come on then let’s go and have a look,” said Big Jones looking over at Alfie and Colin who were killing themselves with laughter, and he thought he knew why.
“I’m not going back in there” said Stumpy.
“Neither am I,” echoed Morgan.

But Big Jones just grabbed hold of Alfie, dragging him out of his sleeping bag and told Morgan and Stumpy that they would go and have a look.
"Where's the owl?" Big Jones asked Alfie.
"I think Colin put it back in the box," he said.
But before he could say another word Big Jones opened the door and all he could see in the darkness were two green eyes staring at him out of the darkness in the corner of the room.
"You told me that the owl was in the box," he said as he too was laughing at the thought of Stumpy waking up to the sight of a pair of green eyes looking down at him from the darkness.
"Must have escaped," came the reply.

Big Jones hurriedly grabbed a blanket and threw it over the owl and made a dive for the bird an international goalkeeper would be proud of and shouted to Alfie to go and get the box. By now Morgan had come back up to the room and when he saw what it was that had frightened him he picked up his shoe and hurled it at Alfie who was laughing at him, but as Alfie moved out of the way the shoe went over his shoulder and hit the blanket Big Jones was holding causing the bird to fall out and fly straight down the stairs and out through an open window never to be seen again.

Chapter 16

The local fire brigade were playing their annual charity rugby match against the local ambulance station and once again they extended an invitation for the boys to be their guests. The game was to be played on a Wednesday afternoon with a 12 o'clock kick off and there was to be refreshments after the game. The boys were not due to go back up to Oxford until the Thursday after the game but King Will arranged for them to go up a day early so that they could support the fire station boys who had been good to them. On the day of the match the boys went down to the local rugby field where the game was to be played and they saw that there was a marquee erected for the game where there was a bar so they had a few drinks before the game.

The captain of the fire brigade came over and asked if any of the boys would like to have a game as they were two players short, so DD and Leighton offered to have a game. The captain came back and had a bag in his hand which he put on the floor and pulled out two pairs of boots and some shorts and socks. Leighton was the first to grab the boots which fitted him leaving DD with a pair of boots which were three sizes too big for him,

"I can't play in these," he moaned.
Before he could say any more Stumpy quipped, "I've seen you play and it makes no difference what you put on, it won't make you any good."
"Go on then mouth, you play," shouted DD.
"Too old now," Stump replied, "but when I was your age I could play barefooted and be better than you."
"I know," replied DD, "boots weren't invented then."
The game started and DD was running around with some newspaper stuffed in his boots and a pair of shorts two sizes too small, which he split when he made his first tackle, which caused hoots of laughter from all the watching boys. When he stopped to change his shorts when there was a break in play this time for a pair that were too big, he took a drink from a bottle that was passed to him, and as he took a large gulp he almost spat it back out as the bottle was filled with homemade cider and not water as he had expected.
I forgot to tell you about the bottle "the captain shouted over to DD "it is a tradition of ours to use a local beverage, rather than water it gives the boys a pick me up".

After the game the boys were all invited back to the local rugby club where there was a buffet laid on and the fire brigade and ambulance men made a collection for the striking miners. The firemen told the boys that they play the ambulance service in a cricket match in the summer and a rugby match in the winter, and the boys were welcome to come to the cricket match even if as they all hoped they were back in work. Alfie remarked that he enjoys watching cricket causing Big Jones to say, "When did you see a cricket match boy? You've always been a rugby boy."
"Went once down to Cardiff," Alfie interrupted.
"Who with?" Big Jones questioned him.
"Went with a West Indian girl I knew," Alfie replied.
"You don't know a West Indian girl boy."
"Shut up and leave me tell you," Alfie went on, "it was in the summer a couple of years back and it was a lovely day and we were sitting on the grass watching the game by the boundary. A West Indies batsman hit a ball for four and it hit the girl right between the legs."
They were all captivated by what Alfie was saying no more than the fireman, who looked at Alfie as he was waiting for him to finish the story, but Alfie stopped talking, so the fireman said wincing as he thought of it,
"That must have been painful!"
"Yes," replied Alfie almost losing his words through laughter, "it was; it broke two of my fingers."

As the afternoon went on there were more stories told, and as the beer started to flow
Howler got up to play the piano which was standing in the corner. Stumpy as usual gave the first song and the firemen and ambulance men and everybody in the club joined in. The Dwarf was sitting by the piano when he decided he had to go to the toilet only to find that as he went to stand up his legs would not support him, and he fell over landing on the piano knocking Howler's pint off the top of the piano and into the inside of the piano.
Howler bet Alfie £5.00 that he could not eat six pepper sandwiches without a drink.
"What do you mean by pepper sandwiches?" he asked.
"Well just six pieces of bread with pepper in them and nothing else."
"Easy," said Alfie, "go get them."

Howler came back with six pieces of bread and a pot of pepper and he put the pepper on to the bread and gave them to Alfie.
Alfie started to munch away and he had soon finished five of the sandwiches, when he was a little red in the face and half way through the last sandwich Big Jones picked up his drink and turned to Alfie and said, "I think this beer you bought me is sour; taste it for me," as he put it by Alfie.
Alfie put the sandwich down and picked up the beer and took a drink from the glass, as he did Howler came rushing forward waving his arms and shouting, "I won the bet, I won the bet, I said six sandwiches without a drink."
Alfie looked over at Big Jones who was standing there with a wicked grin on his face and he knew he had been set up.
"Come on boy you've had enough, we had better take you back to the college," Big Jones said as he picked the Dwarf off the floor. "Can anyone get us a taxi?"
One of the locals in the club shouted across.
"No need for a taxi, I'll phone my brother, he's got our works transport, and he'll take you home. And with that he went off to phone. "He'll be here as soon as he can; he's just down the town on a spot of business so have another drink and I'll let you know when he's here."

Sure enough the man kept his promise and the boys were told that the man's brother was outside waiting for them. Leighton and Big Jones were the biggest of them all and they lifted the dwarf off the chair and carried him out of the club with his legs dangling and his head on his chest like some sort of broken rag doll. When they got outside the club they could not believe their eyes. Stepping out of the club they

expected a van, as they were told that there was room for them all, but to their amazement what was waiting for them was a hearse, and the driver was still dressed in his undertaking clothes.
As he stepped out of the car he said, "Come on then, put him in the back and I'll get you lot back to the college."

The boys just looked at each other not knowing what to do as a crowd had gathered from the club knowing what the man's business was, so they just lifted the dwarf into the back of the hearse and as they did he just fell backwards. As he lay there motionless DD got into the back and folded the dwarf's arms across his chest and told the driver to go as the rest of the boys got into the hearse.

On the way back to the college they had a lot of strange looks at what seemed like a dead body just lying there in the back of the hearse, and when the driver had to stop at a set of traffic lights on a junction by the river two people on push bikes were looking stunned at the sight in the back of the hearse that they almost went over the river bank.
The following morning Big Jones was first to wake up followed by Alfie and they decided to go for a walk to get rid of their hangover from the previous night. As they walked down into the town they walked past a pet shop when Alfie stopped and turned to Big Jones.
"Did DD say that he forgot his shampoo?"
"Yes, but he can buy his own," came the reply in a slightly startled tone,
"Don't be nasty," Alfie told his big pal as he disappeared into the pet shop and emerged with a paper bag in his hand.
"What have you got there boy?" enquired Big Jones.
"Shampoo, but not any old shampoo; this is special," sniggered Alfie as he pulled out the bottle to reveal extra strong dog shampoo.
"If he wants to wash his hair today, he can use this."

On the way back Alfie again stopped this time at a chemist, where he bought a bottle of ordinary shampoo.
As they made their way back to the college Alfie persuaded Big Jones to mention to DD that his hair looked dirty,
"Why don't you tell him?"
"Because he will think I'm up to something"
"But you are."
"I know but he doesn't know that."

Back at the college the rest of the boys were now awake and as usual DD was not in a good mood. Alfie meanwhile went into the bathroom and emptied shampoo out and put the dog shampoo into the ordinary shampoo bottle.

"Look at the state of you boy," Big Jones said, "You look awful, and your hair is like a shabby sheepdog."
Big Jones knew that DD was very vain about his hair and that he would take the bait.
"I forgot my shampoo when I came up here so I can't wash it."
Alfie shouted across, "I've got some, and if you ask nicely I'll sell you a bit."
"What do you need shampoo for lollipop ball head?" he grunted to Alfie.
"Never mind why I've got it, do you want a bit?"
The temptation of being able to wash his hair seemed too much to resist, so DD asked Alfie and he was given the shampoo. As DD went into the bathroom to have a shower Alfie and Big Jones were laughing, and they told them what Alfie had done.
"Give him time to get in the shower and we'll have a bit of fun," Alfie said with a smirk on his face.

As they waited they heard DD getting into the shower and Alfie crept into the bathroom and he could see DD in the shower through the frosted glass panel on the shower cubicle. He crept in and took his towel off the hangar it was on and moved back and bent down by the water stop tap and waited for DD to put the shampoo on his hair. When DD put the shampoo on his hair it produced a fierce lather and the more that DD tried to wash it off the more it lathered up. It was at this point that Alfie turned the cold water off causing DD to scream and try to get out of the shower, but with all the lather covering his head and face he could not see where his towel was to wipe his face and he had to feel his way along the wall. Just as he got to the end of the wall Alfie turned the cold water back on and watched as DD tried frantically to rinse the shampoo off his hair.

Alfie quickly moved forward and picked the shampoo bottle up and reached up and poured the rest of the bottle over the top of the shower on to a helpless and unsuspecting DD causing even more lather. He then moved back and once again turned the cold water off causing DD to scream again and once again try to find his towel when Alfie again turned the water back on. This happened over and over until Alfie could no longer contain his laughter.
With DD screaming as the cold water was turned on and off time and again.
"Whoever you are I'll tear your head off when I catch you," he screamed as he tried to rinse the shampoo from his head and the suds out of his eyes.

When DD finally emerged from the shower his skin was all red and

blotchy and his eyes were red and puffed up. “Who’s the comedian?” he screamed, as he tried to find out who was responsible for turning the water on and off, but nobody said a word.
“What shampoo did you use boy?” said Big Jones, “Because it left a lovely shine on your hair.”
“Never mind the shine; I’m burning all over, that shower was scalding hot!”
“Why didn’t you put some cold water on as well then?” Big Jones said trying to hide his laughter.
“I did but one of you lot kept turning the cold water off, and when I find out who it was I’ll hit them so hard that when they wake up their clothes will be out of fashion.”

Chapter 17

The rest of the week went by without too much happening and there was still no news of any meeting between the coal board and the union, causing a bit of frustration to be creeping in to some of the areas that once were solid behind the strike.

At the vale colliery where the boys worked, there was another man who crossed the picket line and this was followed by another two the following week making a total of six in all. These men, or scabs as they were better known, were escorted into the colliery every day and then spent the next seven hours sitting in the offices. Some of the miners at the vale were friendly with some of the police officers who were used to escort the scabs into the colliery. Indeed Alfie knew a few police officers who played rugby for the club that he followed every Saturday, and they used to tell the boys that they did not like taking these people across the picket lines, but they were only doing as they were told, as one officer told Alfie one Saturday afternoon in the rugby club after the game that some police officers had indeed refused to take these scabs over the picket lines, but the only ones who were excused were the ones who had family members who were involved in the strike.

There were also rumours that the army were also being used to break the strike, indeed at one rally that was organised in Cardiff it was rumoured that one miner came face to face with his brother, but that rumour was never proved, although there was a time that once on the march in London that Big Jones stood in front of a police officer and as he looked down at him he could see him shaking and sweating, as he looked up at the man mountain standing in front of him, Big Jones noticed that he did not have any number on the arm of his jacket.

Although some of the police officers at home and around the country were generally sympathetic to the miners cause there were the odd few who tried to make life awkward. There was one time that the Dwarf was sitting down on a bench minding his own business and having a cigarette when these two police officers came up to him and one of them said with a smirk on his face,
"Do your feet go up to the top of those shoes boy?" referring to the winkle picker shoes that the dwarf liked to wear, but the reply they received left them stuck for words.
"No officer, but tell me does your head go to the top of that helmet?" And he calmly got up off the bench with the cigarette still in the corner of his mouth as it usually was and walked away sniggering to himself at the way he shut him up.

It was decided by the union leadership in Cardiff that a mass picket would man the gates of the Vale colliery on the Monday morning to try and stop the scabs from going into the colliery. King Will said that he had organised about a hundred men to attend who were mostly local men who could walk to the colliery and that mini buses were to be used to pick up the men who were not local as the police would be on the look-out for a lot of cars travelling together, and that word was not to get out as if the police found out they would try to stop the men from going.

On the Monday morning the boys met outside the local club at 4.30 am for the mini bus to pick them up to take them to the colliery to picket the scabs going into the colliery.
As the boys were travelling in the mini bus which was driven by Jaimie they were asked if they had told anybody about where they were going, and they all said that they had not mentioned anything to anybody
"Great "said Jaimie "the less the police know the better"
But as the bus entered the next village to the vale it became apparent that the police had found out about what was happening, because as they approached the square in the village there was a police van parked in a side street and as they got to the square a police inspector was standing in the road waving a torch with around another 50 or 60 officers standing behind him.

Jaimie stopped the mini bus and wound the window down to talk to the officer.
"Can I help you officer Jaimie asked.
"Yes can you tell me where you are going at this time of the morning "said the inspector in what was thought to be a Cardiff accent.
"Why is there a law against people in mini buses "replied Jaimie.

The police inspector looked at Jaimie with slightly angry look on his face

"All depends where you are going "he said "but if you are going to the vale colliery I will ask you to turn back"

"I was under the impression that this is a free country and there were no travel restrictions here" replied Jaimie who by now was starting to get irritated by the officer's attitude

"Just do yourself a favour boy and turn the van around before I will have you arrested for obstructing a police officer in his duty.

By now Jaimie had his stubborn head on and he was refusing to turn the van around, when a car pulled up behind them and King Will stepped out,

"What is the problem here "he asked,

and with Jaimie and the police officer trying to talk at the same time King Will asked Jaimie to go back into the van while he spoke to the officer.

"I believe that these men are going to the Vale colliery and it is my job to stop them "said the officer to King Will,

"On what grounds "King Will asked "as controlled, peaceful picketing is not illegal in this country."

The police inspector was furious but was not to be outdone.

"Okay you are correct but I don't think that the mini bus is roadworthy, and I will have to have a ministry of transport officer to come here and have a look at it"

"How long that take will "asked King Will, knowing that the officer was not going to do him any favours.

"All depends when I can get somebody here, but they don't start work until 9.0'clock so ask the driver to park the van up somewhere safe" he replied with a smug look on his face.

King Will knew that there was no way that the mini bus was going to go anywhere and that the officer would make things as difficult as possible for them all so he told Jamie to tell the boys to get out of the mini bus and he could it back 200 yards up the road where there was some waste land where they could leave the van and they would all have to walk to the Vale, which was about 2 miles away. By now another mini bus had been stopped by the police so the two mini buses were all parked on the waste land and everybody started to walk.

In all fairness to King Will he offered to send the car he was in back and walk with the boys but he was told that he should go on ahead, and tell the rest the men who were there what had happened.

As they all started to walk the police were following at a distance watching everything that was going on. It took about half an hour for most of them to reach the colliery and as they went down the hill and turned the corner by the garage on the end of the street they stopped in amazement at what they could see.

About a hundred people were standing opposite the colliery gates, and as they looked up towards the mountain behind the terrace housing all that they could see was torches shining brightly in the morning gloom with men making their way over from the next valley.
King Will was standing by the colliery gates talking to some police officers and as the boys got closer to him they could hear him saying that he had no idea where these men were coming from as he had only organised about eighty men. One police officer told him that it was totally illegal for this amount of people to attend a picket, and he was correct as King Will knew that only six people were allowed on a picket line at any one time, so he got up on the wall and shouted
"Can you all move back and do not obstruct the gates or the police officers".
Which he might as well have said in a foreign language as nobody moved anywhere, as the people who were coming over the mountain started to arrive on the scene the crowd was starting to swell and fill the narrow road between the colliery and the houses and it was starting to get unmanageable for the police to control.
The inspector in charge told King Will
"If this gets any worse I will have to call for reinforcements"
To which King Will replied
"If you stop the scabs from coming in to work I will try and get the crowd to disperse"
The officer did not answer but he turned around and went into the colliery office and after around ten minutes he returned and called King Will over to him and said that he" could not stop anybody going into work."

The local boys and the people who worked in the colliery were looking around and there were a lot of faces that they did not recognise and it seemed that most of the people there had nothing to do with the colliery. Big L made a comment to King Will that he thought that some of the people there did not have any connection with the dispute and were there just to cause trouble, and he was soon to be proved correct, as a young man with short cropped hair threw a stone at one of the police officers which just missed his head and quickly disappeared into the crowd, this caused anger amongst the men who worked at the colliery as they did not want violence, and they knew that was not the way to get public support. There was still a lot of pushing and shouting going on and you could feel the tension as it became apparent when the police formed a line between the men and the road that the scabs were on their way.

A police car came speeding down the road followed by a police van and another car hurriedly turned into the colliery. This caused a mass push as the men tried to stop the van from going in to the colliery, but the police held their line firmly, but some of the strangers in the crowd were intent on causing trouble and soon they were surging forward towards the police line and some were behaving in an aggressive manner which was not what King Will or the men who worked there wanted.

One man came charging through the heaving mass carrying what seemed like a lump of wood and hurled it at the line of police hitting one of them in the chest causing him to fall to the ground, this was met with shouts of disapproval from the genuine men with again King Will appealing for everybody to keep calm. Alfie was in the middle of the crowd and as the pushing got worse he stumbled and lost his balance causing one of his shoes to come off and he was lucky not to go down on the floor only for big Jones to catch him by his collar and drag him up. The police were by now starting to throw their weight around and as they saw one of their colleagues go down injured they started to lash out with their truncheons at anybody who came within range. One totally innocent man who was pushed towards the police line was hit over the head with a truncheon causing a large gash to open on his head, and he was dragged away and bundled into a van. This caused another man to rush forward shouting
"that's my brother and he has done nothing" but as he was protesting he was set upon by three police officers who were all brandishing their truncheons and also punching the man, and he was hurled into the back of another van,where he could be heard shouting and kicking the inside of the van.

All around there were fights breaking out between the police and the crowd who were now resembling a mob more than a peaceful as was intended,as Alfie looked around he heard a familiar voice that he recognised as that of Leighton and saw that had a boy of about twenty years old by the throat,
"what's the matter"asked Alfie,
"he was going to throw a brick through the window of the house behind him" replied the man mountain "but I caught him in time"
Leighton kept hold of the boy and dragged him by the throat to the back of the crowd and told him that if he saw him again that he would hit him back over the mountain where he had come from,the boy took the hint and ran as fast as he could back up the steps away from the

colliery.Things eventually started to quieten down and the crowd dispersed as quickly as they had arrived leaving only the men who worked there and some of the local people left there.
King Will approached the police inspector and complained about the way the police handled the situation but he was told that the situation got out of hand when the lump of wood was thrown at one of his officer's.

It was rumoured a few weeks later that the whole thing was a set up by the union leadership in Cardiff who leaked information to other lodges that were far more militant than they were in the Vale, so that they could get more men there to have a show of strength and test the resolve and resources of the police,and to try to find out if they were using army personnel. This was never proved despite King Will going the Cardiff office to complain.
The Vale workers continued to picket the colliery every day but there was never another incident that morning which left men nursing cuts and bruises.

Chapter 18

Colin Asthma's son was getting married and Big Jones, Alfie and Stumpy were all invited to the wedding. Alfie and Big Jones along with their wives decided not to go to the wedding service but instead they would go straight to the club where the reception was to be held. On arriving they decided to go into the lounge for a drink and wait for the rest of the wedding party to arrive.

"Let's stay here for a bit until the speeches have been made and then we can go upstairs for the buffet," Big Jones whispered to Alfie.
"Not a bad idea," Alfie replied, "we'll be bored anyway."
After about an hour Alfie went upstairs and looked into the hall and he could see people starting to go up to the buffet table. Alfie went back down the stairs and told Big Jones that the formalities had finished and that the buffet had started, so they went up to the hall. Big Jones went in first and found a table at the back of the hall while Alfie went to get some drinks.

"Go on girls, go get some food before it is all gone," said Big Jones as he cast an eye around the hall.
"I can't see Stumpy," he told Alfie as he came back.
"You know what he's like, he'll probably be late," came the reply.
The two wives came back and Big Jones and Alfie were soon devouring the food that was brought to them by their wives. As the

food went Big Jones said that he was still hungry but nobody would go to the buffet table so he went up for more food. As he was on his way up he noticed that there were a lot of people that he didn't know and he still could not see Stumpy, and he also realised that he could not see Colin Asthma anywhere and he did not recognise many other people. As he was on his way to the buffet he spotted a committee man and he went over to him and asked, "Where's Colin?" Big Jones asked the man.
"Preparing his son's wedding," he replied with a puzzled look on his face.
"What do you mean preparing his son's wedding? This is his son's wedding."
"Well if I were you I would check your invite, Colin's son is not getting married until tomorrow," the man told him.
Big Jones went back to the table and told Alfie and their wives what he had been told, and they checked their invitation and sure enough they were in the wrong wedding, and Colin's son was getting married the following day but as they were there they decided to stay, but their wives had other ideas and they had to go home and go to the wedding the following day.

On the Wednesday the boys were on their way back up to Oxford and Stumpy could not wait to tell everybody about Big Jones and Alfie going to the wrong wedding,and all the way up they had to put up with the various wise cracks, with DD saying, "If brains were made of gun powder Alfie and big boy wouldn't have enough to blow their hats off."

As they were driving along they decided to stop off at the farm to buy some bacon and cider. When they were driving up the lane to the farm there were some horses in the field opposite,
"I bet I could ride that brown gelding," Alfie said.
"You've got a job to walk, never mind ride a horse," said DD.
"Watch this then fat boy," said Alfie as Lou stopped the minibus for them to get off.

With that Alfie was over the fence and was running up the field towards the horses. The rest of the boys were standing by the edge of the field and where the dwarf was standing there was a ditch, Stumpy walked behind the dwarf and gave him a playful push, but the dwarf lost his footing and fell into the ditch. As they were all laughing at Alfie trying to catch the horse Stumpy shouted across.
"Quick come here! The dwarf is going down into the mud," which caused more laughter, but Big Jones could tell by Stumpy's tone of voice that he was not joking. As Big Jones went over he could see that

the dwarf was down to his knees in the mud and he was shouting to the boys to get him out.
"Leave him there until we come back and we can pick him up on the way home," shouted DD, but Big Jones and Stumpy went to the edge of the ditch and managed to reach out and catch hold of the dwarf's outstretched hands and pull him out of the bog-like mud minus a shoe. As he stood on the grass verge he was complaining how Stumpy had tried to kill him while the rest of the boys were still laughing, with DD saying that he reminded him of a swamp monster.

With all this going on nobody noticed that Alfie had got on the horse but as everybody turned around and started to shout the horse bolted and started to run at the fence when it suddenly stopped and Alfie went straight over the top of the horse's head and landing head first into a pool of water. As Alfie came limping back down the field in a state of shock, he stood there soaking wet and as he looked at the Dwarf he soon forgot about the events with the horse as he looked at the dwarf covered in a green slime,
"What have you been up to then?" Alfie asked.
"Stumpy tried to kill me," he replied, but before he had a chance to tell Alfie what had happened Lou told the boys to get on the minibus, as he wanted to get out of there before the farmer turned up. They all got on the minibus but as Alfie and the Dwarf went to get on Lou stopped them saying that they had to take their clothes off, as he was in charge of the minibus and if it was dirty he would have to clean it, so Alfie and the Dwarf had to make the rest of the journey back to Oxford in just their underpants.

They finally got back to the college and Alfie accused Lou of going the long way around the town and purposely stopping at the traffic lights for longer than he normally would for people to look inside. Alfie and the dwarf went for a shower and the rest of the boys went to the students' bar. It was while they were there that the subject arose about the time that DD was caught sleeping in work by the manager of the colliery. There was a furious row with DD telling the manager that he was not sleeping, but the manager insisted that he was asleep saying to DD
"Your eyes were closed so you must have been sleeping."
But DD was as sharp as him when he replied, "Yes my eyes were closed, but I had my boots on too but I wasn't walking."
The manager just stood there with his mouth open not knowing what to say, and DD never heard anything again. Alfie and the dwarf came into the students' bar to shouts of: "Here they come: the lone ranger and the swamp monster."
But as usual they just ignored the remarks.

Jamie came in and told the boys that he wanted two volunteers to take some leaflets around the doors that evening and before there was a chance for anybody to volunteer, DD shouted that Big Jones and Alfie were on picket duty until the following afternoon so they should do it. After a bit of a heated discussion they decided to do it, and off they went. Jamie dropped them off in a council estate which was not too far away, and gave them some leaflets to hand out and ask people for support for the miners against the government.

As they went around the estate they were putting leaflets through the letter boxes and a lot of people were coming out of their house and calling the boys back and giving the leaflets back to them and telling them not to come to their door again or they would phone the police about him. Alfie went to put a leaflet through one door and as he approached the door the door suddenly opened and there was a very irate woman standing there, as Alfie gave her the leaflet she threw it back in his face without looking at it and told him to get off her property or she would have them arrested, as he walked away he said quietly in a rather sarcastic tone
"I don't suppose theres any chance of a cup of coffee then?"
The woman must have had ears like a hawk as Alfie could hear her shouting, "I'll have the police on you."

Alfie and Big Jones carried on trying to hand out leaflets without much success when a police car pulled up and called the boys over to their car,
" Listen boys," the officer said, "we've just had a phone call from a woman saying there were two men begging on the street, we know the woman and she is always complaining but her husband is a local councillor so our sergeant has told us to investigate."
Alfie told the officers what had happened and they could see the funny side of it but they asked them if they could leave it for the night, which they did. The officers asked them if they would like a lift but Big Jones told them that they would walk as it was not too far. On the way back they passed a fish and chip shop. Alfie walked inside and asked the man behind the counter if he would like the leaflets to use as chip paper, the man took the leaflets off them and he gave them a bag of chips each in return.
"Come on boy, let's go back and we'll tell Jamie that all the leaflets have been handed out." So they made their way back to the students' bar were the rest of the boys were.
"You weren't long," said Jamie as they walked into the room.
"No, we don't mess about," Big Jones told him.

The students' bar or hall as they used to call it was a busy place with a lot of different nationalities but they gave the miners plenty of welcome, after all this part of the university was sponsored by the T.U.C. and most of the students there were from working class families. This was also where the students came to revise or study if they wanted to get out of the accommodation block. One day a student walked in and Stumpy was sitting there with a paper on the table in front of him. As the student walked past he looked at the paper and he asked Stumpy if that was his usual paper, when he replied that it was, he answered that he found it unusual that he would buy a French paper.

Alfie was sitting in the corner by himself with his feet up on a chair reading the paper when he fell asleep with the paper still in his hands. DD was watching and he asked the dwarf for a lend of his lighter. As he watched Alfie's chin drop on to his chest he quietly crept over to Alfie and set the paper alight. Alfie was awoken by the flames and as he opened his eyes DD threw a jug of water he had brought all over the paper putting the fire out and soaking Alfie. Alfie looked across at all the boys who were laughing and saw the dwarf with his lighter in his hand and blamed him and told him that he had better watch out as he would have his own back.

Chapter 19

The following day word reached the boys that there had been another man who had crossed the picket line at the Vale colliery, making the total scabs now up to seven.Jamie brought the news in as he had been on the phone to King Will, but he had some good news as well.
"There is to be a meeting between the union and the Coal Board this afternoon, so keep your fingers crossed for some good news."
This was the news that everybody was hoping for as a lot of people were starting to think that the strike was now just dragging on a bit too long, and the feeling was that a lot of people and the other unions who had supported the miners since the start of the strike were now of the opinion that with the cold weather now near an end there still seemed to be plenty of coal reserves. The other issue which was turning the public against the miners was the level of violence that was being reported in the media, although the men on the picket lines were also saying that the violent acts were not being caused by the miners but by sources such as the National Front and other militant factions not related to the miners' union.

Another thing that was turning public sympathy against the miners was the media report that miners leaders had met up with representatives of the Libyan government in a Paris hotel. These claims were particularly hurtful to the miners' cause since the murder of a police-woman outside the Libyan embassy in London was still fresh in people's minds although this did not stop the government buying oil from Libya it was claimed in some sources. It was also claimed that the miners' union had accepted money from the Russian miners and this money had been authorised by the Russian government, and the British government claimed to have seen documents that showed that this money was authorised at the highest level.

The other thing that was being used by the government was that the longer the strike carried on the more chances there were that the mines might lose the contracts that they had with the power stations, and as it was being pointed out coal could be imported from as far afield as Australia, America and South America, and with many homes converting to gas and oil and the power stations also being converted they were not totally reliant on coal. The railways also were converting to diesel and electricity, the only power supply sector that was reliant on coal was the C.E.G.B. (Central Electricity Generating Board).

There was also the government's plan called the Rudely plan, which was a scheme to cut Britain's reliance on coal, drawn up by a right wing Conservative MP. There was also the fact that six striking miners died during the course of the conflict, with two of the deaths being viewed as suspicious, and two striking miners being jailed for manslaughter for the incident in South Wales with the taxi. Three teenagers were also sadly killed while they were picking coal from a colliery waste heap.
The effect of the strike was also taking its toll on the miners and their families as due to the fact that the power stations had learnt from previous disputes with the miners and had stockpiled coal, there were no mass power cuts as in previous strikes and the only ones who were with out power were the miners themselves who had no money to pay their power bills.

That afternoon Alfie and Big Jones along with Lou and Colin Asthma went on to the picket, all of them had high expectations that maybe there might be some news from the meeting. The day seemed to drag on and there was nothing happening at the power station making it a long and tedious afternoon.

When they did finish they were picked up by Jamie and he told the boys that the meeting had not been successful. In a news interview the miners' leader said that although the meeting seemed to go well and that they thought that an amicable agreement could be reached, the Coal Board chairman asked for the meeting to be adjourned for an hour. When the meeting resumed the Coal Board chairman seemed to have changed his stance on a number of issues and the meeting broke down. The miners' leaders accused the Coal Board chairman of using the adjournment to contact the British Prime Minister directly to take advice. This was denied, but no reason was given why he had come back to the table with such a negative approach when it looked like a solution to the dispute could be found with both sides making concessions, but on resuming the meeting the Coal Board suddenly refused to make any concessions.

This news dampened the spirits of not only the striking miners but also the women's groups and the wives of the miners who had stood behind their men by attending rallies and standing on picket lines in the cold wet mornings, and organising the various food donations into parcels, and also setting up soup kitchens and raising money with things like sponsored walks, jumble sales and car boot sales. Without these women behind the miners the strike would have crumbled a lot earlier than it did.

Much was also reported in the media about the fact that a lot of mining areas were giving less support to the strike, but again this was played down by the miner's leaders as propaganda by the conservative press.
That evening morale was at a low point as the boys sat and talked with the students. Big Jones, Alfie, DD and Stumpy decided to go for a walk down into the town. On the way into town they passed the vicarage and Alfie noticed that there were some apple trees in the garden with some juicy looking apples.

There was a football match going on and the boys decided to try and get in to watch the game but even though there was only fifteen minutes left they were refused free entry. The boys then decided to go down to the labour club for a pint before walking back to the college While they were in the club they got talking to a West Indian man by the name of Kelly who had befriended them. As they were talking a middle aged couple came over and asked if they were the miners who were staying in the college, the boys told them that they were and the man put a ten pound note on the table and said it was a donation to the strike fund and would the boys mind taking the donation off them.

Alfie was first to react thanking them and telling them that all

donations were welcome and put the money into his pocket. When the couple left the room Kelly told them that they were members of the local labour party and owned a shop in the town.
Alfie pulled the money out of his pocket and got up out of his seat,
"Where are you going boy?" asked Big Jones.
"To get another round of drinks."
"That was a donation for the strike fund and we are on strike." So Alfie was off to the bar and soon reappeared with a tray of drinks and some nuts, and that is where they stayed until the end of the night.
On the way back to the college they went past the vicarage and Alfie stopped by the wall.
"What have you stopped for boy?" said Big Jones in his normal booming voice.
"Look up there at those apples; I don't suppose they will miss a few."
As he was saying it they were over the wall in a flash with Stumpy last over falling flat on his back as he caught his foot on the top of the wall.
"Must have been a small wall for you to catch your foot," said DD laughing as Stumpy got to his feet.

When they got in to the orchard they decided that as Big Jones and DD were the biggest they should go up the tree and Stumpy and Alfie would stay on the ground to pick up the apples. Big Jones and DD climbed the tree and started to shake the branches and surely enough the apples started to fall to the ground. Suddenly the light came on in an upstairs bedroom and Big Jones called down to Alfie and Stumpy to be quiet as he could see the vicar coming into the bedroom. The boys' hearts were beating, like when they were youngsters stealing apples from gardens. Big Jones was giving a running commentary on what was happening, and Alfie and Stumpy were avidly listening to his every word.
"The vicar's taken his collar and coat off and he's looking towards the bedroom door," Big Jones went quiet and Alfie and Stumpy were trying to find out what was happening, but Big Jones kept telling them to be quiet, but they could hear DD laughing. Eventually Big Jones broke his silence.
"The vicar's wife has just walked into his room, and the vicar has got his shirt off. He's pushed his wife against the wardrobe and she's taken her dress off."

With that Big Jones again went quiet and Alfie and Stumpy again were urging him to tell them what was happening. As Stumpy was looking up into the tree Big Jones was still keeping silent when an apple suddenly fell out of the darkness and landed straight on Stumpy's head hitting him between the eyes instantly knocking him

out. Alfie looked down at his mate lying motionless on the floor and shouted up to Big Jones and DD.
"You two had better come down here; I think you've killed Stumpy." Big Jones jumped down from the tree landing on the floor with an almighty thud and he looked down at Stump who was still lying on the floor surrounded by apples. "He's not dead," he said in a quiet tone of voice.
"If it had hit him on the foot he might have been hurt, but his head is as thick as a donkey's dick."

He bent down to try and pick the silver fox up, but as he did DD came over and told Big Jones that he would bring him round. They knew that DD had done a bit of boxing so they both thought that he might know what to do when somebody has been knocked out. But they were both in for a shock as DD stood over Stumpy and urinated all over him saying, "This chance that is too good to miss."
Although this came as a shock to Alfie and Big Jones it had the desired effect as it brought Stumpy around, and he rose screaming to his feet at the sight of DD standing over him in all his glory. As DD turned to run away Stumpy picked up an apple and hurled it at DD but in the darkness he missed and the apple bounced off a tree and hit Alfie on the nose causing him to have a nose bleed.

By now there was so much noise in the garden that they thought that the vicar might have heard, with Big Jones shouting to the boys to get out of the garden in case the police were called; so they scampered over the wall like commandos and got back to the college as fast as they could, leaving all the apples behind them.
When they got to the college DD and Stumpy were still arguing with DD telling him that he should be thanking him as Alfie and Big Jones were going to leave him in the garden, and Alfie moaning about his nose. The dwarf and the rest of the boys were all asking where they had been and how was Stumpy covered in urine, and how did Alfie get a bloody nose, and when Stumpy went for a shower they told them what had happened.

The following morning Alfie, Big Jones and DD were awake before Stumpy, who as usual was still asleep on his mattress and as they spoke about the night before they could all see the funny side of what happened but they thought that they would not say anything to anybody else but keep it to their selves and try not to upset Stumpy, but they knew that the dwarf and the rest of the boys would not be able to resist having a laugh at Stumpy's expense. As Stumpy woke up and came into the room everybody turned around to look at him and burst out laughing. Stumpy had a lump the size of an egg right in

the middle of his forehead and the rest of his forehead was covered in one big bruise.
“Here comes William Tell” shouted the dwarf, but Stumpy was in no mood for any nonsense; he just sat down and asked Alfie to make him a cup of tea.
“Make it yourself,” Alfie retorted.
“But I’ve got a banging headache, and it’s all your fault,” he said feeling sorry for himself.
“How is it my fault? DD threw the apple at you,he told us last night.” This caused DD to shout out at Alfie.
“Don’t tell him that; it was Big Jones that dropped the apple, and anyway it was his fault, because if his mouth was open like it usually is he would have swallowed it.”

Alfie made Stumpy a cup of tea and as he was drinking it he was looking at DD and wondering how he would get his own back.
“Come on let’s go for a walk,” said Big Jones, “so Stumpy can get some fresh air.”
As they walked down out of the college grounds they decided to sit on a bench around the corner from the vicarage, as they were sitting there the vicar walked passed, and as he went past he looked at Stumpy’s head and enquired what had happened to him, but before he could answer Alfie told him that he had had an accident in the garden, and with that he said, “Good morning to you all,” and carried on down the road oblivious to what had happened in his garden.

Later that morning Alfie was sitting on a wall outside of the college when Jamie drove up in the van and asked him how did it go when he was handing the leaflets out.
“Not too bad,” he replied trying to hide the fact that they had not given many out.
“Go and get the big boy,” Jamie requested. “I want you two to come with me, but don’t tell nobody else.”
Alfie went into the college and they came back out to where Jamie was waiting for them.As they drove off they were asking Jamie where they were going but he told them that they would see when they got there.
After a short drive Jamie turned into the estate that they were sent to hand the leaflets out asking people to support the strike, as they looked down the street most of the houses had posters in their windows canvassing for support for the conservative councillors in the local council elections.
“You two must have done well to hand out leaflets down here,” he said with a smirk on his face, and before they could answer him he delivered a killer blow.

"Or were you thinking when you left the leaflets in the fish shop that people could read about the strike when they were eating their chips?"
"Who told you?" asked Alfie.
"I saw the leaflets when I bought chips there last night, but we knew that you would never get any support down here but DD thought it would be fun to send you down here."
As they got out of the van they asked Jamie not to say anything and decided to pay DD back.

That afternoon Alfie and Big Jones went on their usual picket line duty along with Stumpy and the dwarf. The afternoon was fairly quiet and with the exception of the locals who brought them coffee and sandwiches nothing much was happening.The lorries that went into the power stations by now were stopping to talk to the boys, but as usual when they tried to talk to them about not going in they were told the same old story that they had a family to look after, and they had no choice but to do as they were told or there was a lot of men who would take their place. The afternoon seemed to drag on and Big Jones and Alfie spent a lot of time talking about how they would get their own back on DD.

Eventually the minibus arrived and they all got on and made their way back to the college, as they got back they made their way into the building and they were met with the delicious smell of curry.
"Who made the curry?" asked the dwarf.
"One of the students made it and Scottish Ronnie brought it in when you were on the picket line," said DD as he put four plates on the table.
"So get it down you; we had ours this afternoon."
Nobody found that strange as the students were always sending food over for the boys.

As they devoured the food nobody seemed to notice DD was sitting in the corner with a big smile on his face, until the Dwarf turned around and asked him what he found so funny.
"Nothing, I was just thinking that you lot were eating like a load of animals."
To which Colin Asthma and Morgan also started to laugh, but they were more concerned about eating their food so they just took no notice.
Colin asthma made a comment that the lump on Stumpy's head was getting bigger.
"Watch I don't give you lump on your head," Stumpy replied.
"You haven't got a dog's chance," Colin said, and this caused more laughter amongst them all.

Once they had finished their meal there was the usual argument about who was going to wash the plates with Alfie saying that he had done them the night before, but nobody offered so the plates were left on the table. While the rest of the boys played cards Big Jones and Alfie got into their sleeping bags and soon they were fast asleep.
The following morning Alfie and Big Jones went over to the students' union leaving Stumpy and the dwarf in the room alone as the rest of them were out on the power station picket line. Ronnie the Scotsman was there and he got Alfie a cup of coffee and a glass of water for Big Jones and they sat down to have a talk.

Alfie mentioned that they had enjoyed the curry that the students had made.
"What curry?" he asked in astonishment with a puzzled look on his face.
"The beef curry that you brought over yesterday afternoon," Alfie told him.
"I was down in Oxford all day yesterday studying in the library for exams I have got next week, so I didn't see any of your friends, and I don't know of anybody making curry."
Big Jones looked at Alfie and they both thought the same thing: " What was DD up to?"
Saying goodbye to Ronnie they made their way back to the college, still wondering what DD had been up to.

The dirty plates and forks were still on the table and Big Jones picked them up and took them into the kitchen to wash them saying that if he didn't do them nobody would.As he went over to the waste bin to empty the remains of the curry into the bin he noticed some tins,as he put the plates down he took one of the tins out of the bin.
"Alfie, come here!" he shouted.
As Alfie came over to the bin he could see Big Jones holding an empty tin of dog food in his hand and another two tins were still in the bin.
"I knew that he was up to something," Alfie said to the big boy.
"No wonder that he was laughing and saying that we were eating like animals," Big Jones replied, "And asthma head and Morgan must have known."

Stumpy and the Dwarf came over to see what all the noise was about and Alfie showed them the tins of dog food in the bin.
"When I was in the army I ate a dog once so it's no big deal," said the dwarf.

But Stumpy was not amused even though Alfie made a comment that at least it was the best dog food.

"Never mind we are going home in the morning, so we can think of a way to repay those three the next time we come up," Big Jones told the boys.

Jamie came with the van to take the boys out to the power station and on the way he mentioned that DD had told him in the morning about the meal that he had cooked for them the night before, not knowing that they knew what he had put in the curry. When they got to the power station DD, Morgan, Colin and Leighton were waiting for the van.

"How were you lot this morning?"DD asked them.

"Dog rough I suppose," Morgan said before anybody could say a word.

"We know what you did," Big Jones informed them, "so you had better watch out."

"Come on now we don't want a dog fight" Colin asthma mumbled.

As they got into the van DD shouted as it pulled away, "You had better watch Stumpy in case he starts chasing cars."

The rest of the day went by without anymore excitement and the following morning the boys were on their way back home, with the news that there was to be a mass picket at the colliery the following morning.

Five o'clock in the morning a van came to pick the boys up and they were on the way down to the colliery.

About two miles from the colliery they were stopped by the police and told that they could not go any further with the van, and if they wanted to go any further then they would have to walk. It was a cold morning so a brisk walk was not a bad thing, even at this early hour, although not everybody agreed with Stump complaining about the corns on his feet. When they arrived at the colliery they were met with more police and a crowd had already gathered.Alfie looked at the crowd and he did not know a lot of the faces, and there was a lot of hostility, which was unusual, as the vale although being one of the most militant colliery's was not known as having an aggressive stance, indeed King Will had told all his members that any man caught using violence would be removed from all picket duties.

As the police started to line up the crowd pushed forward in expectance of the van bringing the scabs to work arriving. When the van came into sight there was a huge push from behind and Alfie and the rest of his mates were pushed along with the crowd.

As he was pushed along Alfie lost his shoe and if it was not for Big

Jones holding him up he would have fallen to the floor and been trampled by the mass crowd behind him. The van went in through the colliery gates and they were instantly locked and a line of police officers stood along the gates to stop anybody getting through the gates.

There was still a lot of pushing going on but the police seemed to have the crowd under control, until a stone was thrown that hit a police officer cutting his eye. At this point the police were ready to use their batons at any one who remotely looked like using violence until King Will borrowed a loud-speaker from the police and stood on the wall appealing for the violence to stop, saying, "This is a peaceful picket and anybody using violence will not be associated with this lodge."

And he appealed that if anybody knew who threw the stone to help the police to arrest him. All the men who worked in the vale had a lot of respect for King Will and it was not too long before the man who threw the stone was in custody. It later emerged that he was not a miner at all, just a thug out to make trouble.

Everything seemed to be over and the scabs were safely locked away behind the colliery gates and King Will told the boys that they might as wall go home as the police were not going to let anybody near the scabs.

As a gesture the police inspector in charge said that as the miners helped to arrest the thug who threw the stone he would arrange for the minibus that was stopped in the square to come down for the men who needed a lift. As they were waiting for the minibus a man called Handle, who was not a very likeable man, was standing there bragging that although he was on strike he was still making money by working for his brother as a painter on a building site and he didn't care how long the strike went on for as he was earning money.

He was standing on the bottom of the steps by the bridge that went across the river and he was waving a handful of ten pound notes at the boys saying, "Look what I've got. I bet you lot wish you had a stash of cash like this," and he was mocking the boys who had no money

"Why are you here then?" Alfie asked him.

" I've got a job to do down the road so I thought I'd come and see you lot of losers before I go," he sneered.But the smile was soon to be wiped off his face as he didn't know that Big Jones and Leighton, a man who they called the bear, were standing on the steps behind him and they promptly lifted him off his feet, with each of them putting a hand under his arms and threw him and his money into the freezing river, to a very loud round of applause not only from the miners but also by the police officers.

As he emerged from the water he was blue with cold and he turned to the policemen standing there as he screamed at them, "What are you lot laughing for? You should be arresting them for what they have just done to me."
To which one of the officers replied ,"if you had kept your mouth shut, and was not waving your money about then you would not have ended up in the water, so all I saw was you slipping into the water." And as he said that the officer raised his arm and gave Big Jones a huge smile and a thumps up. He later told the boys that he like most of his colleagues were against what the government were doing to the miners, and as like most people in South Wales he had links with the mining industry, but the nature of his job meant that he had to be impartial and he was not allowed to be seen supporting either side, as much as he hated what was being done to the coalfields.

As he walked away drenched with water all that could be heard was the sound of his shoes squelching as he walked.
"That sound is music to my ears," said Alfie.
"That's what they must mean by Handel's water music," said Leighton to the sound of laughter all around him.

Over the next few days word was getting around that in various coal fields men were returning to work, indeed some had returned and took the government's offer of a lump sum payment if they returned to work. This was looked upon as bribery. However the government looked upon it as a break through and made no secret that they thought that the miners who took the bribe as it was called by the N.U.M. were doing so as a protest at the way the strike was being handled by the miners' leaders.

Chapter 20

The Tories were also taunting the miners with an offer of negotiations and then at the last minute cancelling any meeting hoping that more miners would return to work, increasing the pressure on the union. Through all this there was still fight in the die hard miners, men who although they were on the brink of poverty still had their pride and would not accept the fact that if they backed down now there would be the inevitable pit closures and mass redundancies.

Another thing that was met with contempt by the miners was that the government said that the deal that was offered to N.A.C.O.D.S. the colliery officials union was available to the miners was suddenly withdrawn. It seemed that the Tories wanted not to deal with the miners' union but to bring them to their knees. This was also coupled with the words of the Prime Minister when a message was sent to the N.U.M. via the T.U.C., with the chilling words, surrender or else, there were to be no deals, nor surrender by the Tories.

When the miners' leaders chose to ignore these words the T.U.C. openly stated that they had lost all patience with the miners' leaders causing more embarrassment to the N.U.M. leadership.
This message coming after a leading south wales N.U.M. official suggested,"A return to work with no agreement, as the strike was now causing damage to the morale of the miners and the union." This comment was met with anger in South Wales, with men asking, "Why after nearly a year on strike should we go back with no agreement, and the pits would still shut, so we will have spent a year with no wages and go back worse off than when we started."

With all that was being reported in the media the miners were getting more and more disenchanted with the situation and the trickle of men returning to work turned into a steady flow. Another thing was the turning of the newspapers against the strike, the Tories press was always against the miners, but now the labour based papers were starting to turn against the miners; this caused the miners' leaders to turn to the public with an appeal for help, as the T.U.C. it seemed were moving away from the miners: indeed the T.U.C. had never given full support to the miners as they seemed to endorse the government's call for a national agreement which the N.U.M. had constantly refused, but which deep down most miners had wanted a ballot believing that if a ballot had been held the union would have had a mandate for a strike making the strike official and with an all-out strike they would have been in a more favourable position to succeed with their quest to save pits and jobs.

A meeting was called by King Will on a Sunday morning in the club, and all the miners from the vale were urged to attend. King Will told the packed hall that although things seemed bad, it was not a lost cause and this battle could still be won, but those who knew him could see that he knew that the end of the strike was in sight and it was going to be a losing battle, but despite a lot of differing opinions they decided to support the union.

Big Jones, and his mates stayed in the club at the end of the meeting and went downstairs to the bar for a drink before going home, Alfie got a round of drinks and brought them back to the table. Stumpy got up and went to the toilet and when he was gone DD had a sachet of a

liquid laxative which he opened and dropped into Stumpy's beer "That will make him move," he said with a wicked grin on his face. Stumpy came back and sat down and picked up his beer and took a long sip saying, "I've been looking forward to that all morning." Not to be outdone Big Jones lifted his glass to his mouth and drank his pint down in one go.
"Come on then boy,how thirsty are you?" he said trying to get Stumpy to finish his drink.

Big Jones went to the bar carefully keeping Stumpy's glass separate from the rest of the glasses. When he came back he put the drinks on the table and as Stumpy went to pick up his glass he suddenly put it down and made a dash for the toilet, leaving the boys all laughing with the exception of Stumpy.
"Why don't you take your coat off boy?" Big Jones asked him as he was complaining of being warm.

Stumpy got up to take his coat off and as he did Lou noticed that there was a stain on his braces at the back and it had left a dark brown coloured cross shaped stain on the back of his shirt.
Lou made eyes at Alfie and pointed at Stumpy's back. Alfie got up and made an excuse that he was going to see somebody and went behind Stumpy, as he stood behind Stumpy he could instantly detect where the strange smell was coming from and what had caused the stain on Stumpy's shirt.

Alfie sat down by Big Jones and whispered in his ear that when Stumpy went to the toilet in his rush to get his trousers down he must have left his braces hanging down the toilet, but they decided not to let him know, and much to DD's amusement they left him in ignorance of what was on his shirt, despite getting a lot of funny looks and people avoiding him.
When he returned he was looking a little pale but he never had much colour anyway,in fact the only time he ever had a sun tan was during the summer of the strike
Stumpy was always immaculately dressed, never going out with out a tie, and today was no exception.
As he sat down he turned to Alfie and said, "I think you had better go and sit on the toilet, because you smell."

Alfie looked at him and told him that he hadn't done anything, so he started to accuse them all, but nobody owned up to the strange aroma that was hanging around.
It was quite warm in the club despite it being winter, and most of the people had their coats off except Stumpy who kept his on all day.

It was decided that the picketing of the power station would be maintained and the following morning Big Jones and the rest of the boys got into the van driven by Jamie and made their way back up to Oxford to picket the Didcot power station, knowing that the end of the strike was in sight. That evening they went into the students' bar as usual not so much for a drink but for somewhere to relax. While they were there they got talking to the students as they usually did and they were told to go and have some food which they did. Alfie was the last one to come in and as he walked in he saw a packet of cigarettes and a box on the table, thinking that they were Stumpy's he opened the packet and took two out and carefully broke the heads off two matches and planted them in the top of the cigarettes putting the tobacco back so as to make it look normal.

When they had all had their food Alfie waited for Stumpy to have his customary smoke after his food, to his horror he watched as Stumpy reached into his pocket and pulled out his cigarettes and a lighter, Alfie had picked up the dwarf's cigarettes instead, but worse was to come.

There were a group of female students who came to sit opposite them. The Dwarf was soon on his feet and cosying up to the girls. Alfie was looking on as he could see the dwarf picking up his cigarettes and offering them to the girls, only one took up his offer and Alfie watched as the dwarf took out a match from the box and lit it and gave the girl a light. It was all Alfie could do as he watched the dwarf trying to be so gentleman like to stop from laughing as he knew what to expect, as the girl took a puff of her cigarette. exploded as the match caught the burning tip, the girl jumped up and screamed as her eye brows were caught by the flame, causing her friend to throw a drink over her, the dwarf and the girl both rose to their feet together and as the girl looked across at him she screamed abuse at him and lashed out catching the Dwarf on the side of the head, knocking him over the stool he was sitting on causing his false teeth to tumble out of his mouth, chipping the front tooth. Alfie just looked on saying nothing as the rest of the boys went to see if the girl was all right and helping her to her seat.
The dwarf tried to apologise and offer to buy her another drink but the girl just wanted to be left alone, and told him to go away before she went for her boyfriend, leaving him to wonder what had happened, but Alfie never told him.

Chapter 21

The following morning it was reported that an N.U.M. special conference was to be called on March the 3rd.
Many miners were hoping that this conference the eighth since the strike began would be the last, as one miner was reported to have said, "It's OK for the leadership to say fight on but it is us who are being starved back to work not the employers, or the union bosses, and ever since the union have had their funds frozen things have got worse."
The meeting went ahead on 3rd March 1985 and a return without an agreement was proposed by the South Wales delegates, despite knowing that many South Wales miners were against this proposal.
The president and the executive objected to this proposal, stating that half of the workforce were still on strike, and also they wanted the miners who had been sacked during the campaign to be reinstated.
However the delegates were afraid that if a return to work was not voted for it would only mean that the scab element of this strike would only increase and this once great and proud union would crumble,so after a vote was taken a result of 98 to 91 in favour of a return to work was recorded, so the miners returned to work starved and bruised but still defiant and vowing to fight for their seven hundred sacked colleagues through area negations.

Once the vote was taken the national executive urged their members to return to work as a unit with their heads held high on Tuesday March the 5th 1985 after almost a year on strike, although some areas did not go back until a week later.

So the greatest strike in British working history was over. Nobody involved in the strike would ever know how close the government were to defeat, or the cost to the country in their desire to bring the miners down to their knees. Some newspapers estimated the cost to the country in excess of five billion pounds almost bankrupting the country, and in doing so they built up an everlasting hatred for them by the working class of the country, although they will use this defeat to gloat about her triumph there were still people in the ruling classes who behind closed doors would say that the working class people can never be kept down and if another great dispute was to arise the Prime Minister would struggle for support.

Tuesday March 5th 1985 at five o'clock in the morning the miners of the vale gathered outside the community centre a five minute walk from the colliery gates. King Will got up on the bench that was brought as a temporary stage and made a short emotional speech.
"Boys I know how hard it has been for you and I am proud of each and every one of you. This morning we go back to work not as a beaten force with our heads bowed but with our heads held high. We

took on a government that was determined to break the miners, they had prepared for this strike and they did not care about the financial cost or the cost to human lives, or the communities involved in mining.
All that they cared about were their own egos and not a thought about the British working class.That was evident when they brought in an American to do a hatchet job on the steel works first, then when he had run them down to the ground he was told to do the same to the miners, their attitude was there was to be no deals or compromise: the miners must be beaten at all costs, but we have not been beaten, and the fight will continue."

There was a loud cheer and King Will was lifted shoulder high off the bench, as he was visibly shaken and was clearly in tears. The miners marched back to work behind the vale N.U.M. flag, which was carried by Leighton and Big Jones through the crowd of local people who had turned out to support the miners on their return to work just as they had supported them during the strike.

As everybody changed into their working clothes the talk was the same, everybody said: "No more strikes."
The winding gear was soon moving taking the miners down into the bowels of the earth with the no more strikes words still prominent on everybody's lips, as they made the long walk to the coal face, that was until they reached the lamp station where they were to be met by the colliery deputies.

On the way in they had to walk past the scabs who had been taken down the mine earlier, a lot of the miners just ignored them, while others made comments and there were a few who spat at them.
When the face workers were told that they had to go and work with the scabs they all refused.Howler was the team captain and he told the overman in charge that he did not want any scab in his team.
This refusal was relayed to the manger who sent a message down, after telephoning the Coal Board offices in Cardiff, that they had to work with the scabs, or returnees as he called them or they could go home, which they did, so despite "the no more strikes for me" promise they were back on strike two hours later.

When Howler and his team got to the pit surface and had a shower and changed into clean clothes King Will met them outside the pit head baths, and told them all to go into the canteen and wait for him while he met with the manager. On his return he told them that he had seen the manager and that he was adamant that they must work with the scabs, and if anybody did anything to them they would be instantly dismissed. Also the miners' agent and a South Wales executive would be coming to the vale that afternoon to talk to them.

That afternoon they all returned to the colliery and were told to go to the community centre where they were met by King Will, the miners agent, and a man dressed in a neat suit, who they thought was a union representative.

King Will was first to his feet on the stage and gave a brief report of what the manager told him, which was basically what he had told them earlier, and then introduced the miners' agent to the waiting crowd.
As he rose to his feet to a round of applause, they were all expecting words of support, but they were never going to come, as he opened with a short and sharp few words
"Boys what you have done today is stupid bordering on insanity; if you want to keep your jobs, go back to work immediately, because you are playing into the Coal Board's hands. I am not going to say anymore but I am going to let the gentleman on my left explain to you what will happen."

And with that he introduced the man in the suit as the deputy director of the South Wales coal board.
"Gentlemen," he said in a public school accent, "I will make this short and sweet for you, if you do not return to work immediately then I will recommend that this colliery will be closed instantly. Furthermore if this action is undertaken you will all be removed from your jobs, and the men who returned to work earlier and supported the Coal Board will be transferred to an area of their choice. So that is all I am going to say; the matter is in your hands," and with that he got down off the stage and left the hall.

The miners' agent got back to his feet and told the silent crowd that what the man had said was true and not to take his words lightly, and urged the men to go back. These word also were supported by King Will who added, "Boys go back, you all know how I feel about these scabs, and I was with you all of the way through the strike and you know how much I respect you all for what you went through. But I have been in meetings all day with the manager, who in all fairness is a good man, but as he told me in private that although he agreed with the principle of what you are saying, his hands were tied as soon as you walked through the gates."

So that night the miners returned to work at the vale. Going back in some ways was a relief as they could now try and put the hardships of

the last year behind them and go forward and earn some money and repay all the people who had helped in their struggle.
The scabs were given a terrible time by some men, while others totally ignored them, these included emptying their water jacks, and refusing to ride in the cage taking them up or down the pit, but one of the most hurtful things was when one man they called Cuffy sat down by a scab as he was sitting alone having his food, and looked him in the eye and said, "Don't forget you can never hide from what you did and you must live with being a scab, but your children will also be known as scabs, what a legacy to pass on to them."
And with that he got up and walked back to the rest of his mates, leaving the scab alone and with his head bowed.

Chapter 22

The next few months things were hard as the Coal Board brought in new managers and under managers, who were more hardliner than before the strike. Many of these were just out of university and college and had mining degrees which looked good on paper, but in practice they did not have a clue.

There was one manager who owned a farm, who was more concerned about selling potatoes than running the mine. In fact the men nick named him Mr. Potato-head, due to the fact that he would drive on to the yard in the mornings with a trailer full of potatoes on the back of his Land Rover.

Another manager one day came into the coal face and as he entered the face one of the men was on his knees using a shovel, his name was Bailey, but he was known as Bill to all his mates and he was a real character. As the manager walked past him he looked down at Bailey and sneered, "How long have you been working underground then boy?"
Bill Bailey didn't even look up at him, he just turned his head slightly towards him and spat a mouthful of tobacco juice by the side of his foot and said, "Before you were born boy, now go on your way," and he just carried on shovelling.

The following morning Bill Bailey had to go and see the manager before he went down the pit, and explain his actions of the previous day. When he went into the office Howler went with him as the face representative. The manager wanted to suspend Bailey but as Howler put it to him, to do something like that he had to have a witness, and there ten men who were there who heard nothing,so Bailey walked out a lucky man.

Things like this were becoming more frequent across the coal fields, with reports that men had been dismissed in other areas for things like fighting, especially in areas where there were a lot of scabs present.

The vale colliery remained open for a further four and a half years after the strike ended, closing on the 25th of August 1989, along with another mine three miles from the vale and a pit in Kent.

During the time the mine was open the miners did all that they could to keep the mine open.

On the day the vale was closed the union were summoned to a meeting at the Coal Board head office just outside Cardiff.During the meeting they were told that they were only called to the meeting for a review of how the colliery was doing in relation of the out put of coal and the expectant time scale of how long the pit would be kept open for. An engineer told them,"The vale colliery is geologically very good and there are plenty of coal reserves which have not yet been explored, so the life expectancy is very good, in fact I can say that I think that there will be very few pits still open in the country when your pit has to close."

These words were like a breath of fresh air to the union representatives and they left the meeting with a spring in their step as they headed back up to the vale to give the workforce the good news. Half way up the motorway the mood suddenly changed as the news came over the radio.

"There has just been an announcement," the news reader said, "by the head of the South Wales Coal Board, the Vale colliery will be closed with immediate effect."

Jamie was driving and he immediately turned the car around and headed back to Cardiff.When they got back to the office they were told that there was nobody there to see them and they were not allowed past the reception area, as security guards ushered them off the premises.

The following morning as the men turned up for work they were met by coal board representatives who told them to go and empty their lockers of any personal belongings.

They all then had to go into the canteen where they were told that they would be informed of what was to happen next. Three men entered the canteen flanked by the manager and under manager, and identified themselves as Coal Board employees. One of them got to his feet and told the men that a decision had been made to close the

colliery.
When they were asked why was the lodge told that the pit was safe, they just replied that a decision had been made at the highest level and that they could not answer any questions, but they told the men that any man who wanted to transfer to another colliery would be allowed to do so and they would get an upheaval payment. They also told the men that if anybody did not want to transfer then they could have a redundancy payment.
Whoever decided to take redundancy did not have to rush and they could take their time to think it over, "As long as you let us know by six o'clock this evening."
With that they left the canteen leaving the men stunned and bitter, as they discussed what they were going to do.
"I've had enough," Alfie told Big Jones. "I'm taking the money, how about you?"
"Same as you boy, why go elsewhere to be treated like dogs?" replied his big friend.

So they went over to the office to join in the queue. There was a lot of clerical workers taking details of who was transferring and who was taking redundancy and the queue soon went down. Alfie entered the room and gave his name and registration number and he made a comment that after all the years he had worked at the vale all he was was a number, but he did not get an answer, as the clerk put three pieces of paper in front of him.
"What are these?" he asked.
The clerk replied, "The first one is a print out of all the days you missed for industrial action, the 72 strike, the 74 strike, and numerous one day disputes you were involved in, so these will be taken out of your redundancy payment." The clerk sat in stony silence as Alfie looked on. "The second document," he continued, "is that you will waive away any claim to the thirteen weeks in lieu of wages earned."
Alfie was fuming as he got off his chair.
"I am not signing that," he said through gritted teeth.
"Well if that is how you feel then I can't make you sign, but if you want to transfer I can arrange it for you".
That was the last thing Alfie wanted so he was left no choice but to sign the documents.
As soon as the two documents were signed the clerk then put the third document on the table, which was the official redundancy document which was signed and then the clerk put the three documents in his brief case and wished Alfie all the best and called the next man in.

Another instance of how they were treated came one Christmas time. The manager asked if some of the men would work over Christmas as

work was behind on the opening of a new coal face. Some men offered to work, which included Christmas Day but told the manager that they wanted treble time, to work the Christmas break which was a week. The manager told them, "It will be all right; these jobs have got to be done."
The men worked over Christmas and completed the job that they were asked to do. The following week when they got their pay docket they had only been paid single time. Thinking that there must have been a mistake they went to see the manager, who told them that there had been no mistake.
"But you said that it will be all right," the men said in unison.
"I know what I said," he replied, "but I did not say I was going to pay you."
And with that he asked them to leave his office as he was expecting a telephone call.

Another instance when there was lucky escape for some of the work force was when a rat was put into an empty powder tin and sent up the pit during a night shift. When the powder tin was opened the following morning the rat leapt put of the tin and leapt over the shoulder of the man who opened the tin.
Word got back to the manager who was furious at this prank, and he vowed to find out who did this. There was an enquiry at the pit but nobody knew anything and the culprits were never found out, although it was common knowledge who had done it.
The manager also knew who had put the rat into the powder tin, but as he told King Will, "I know who it was and so do you, but you know I can't prove it but if I ever get any proof I will sack them on the spot."
From that time on all powder tins were numbered, and they had to be signed for.

Another instance of the dirty tricks that the Coal Board used was to knock down the washeries where the coal was cleaned and build a new one, although the washeries were fairly new, at a cost of nearly half a million pounds, along with building a new lamp room and offices for the manager and other officials.
The reason the Coal Board gave was that they were investing for the future, but in reality they were spending money so that they good say that the colliery was working at a loss and was not viable.

Just before the pit shut Alfie and his wife were on a plane going on holidays when somebody tapped him on the shoulder. As Alfie turned around he could see sitting behind him was the manager of the pit when they went back after the strike. He was an old fashioned sort of manager who started work in the mines as a young man and worked his way up to be a manager by going to night school and getting a mining engineer's degree and working his way through the ranks. Alfie asked him if it was correct that he was sacked after the strike as rumour had it.

His reply shocked Alfie as he told him, "After the strike all the managers and under managers were told by the Coal Board directors in each area that they were not to tolerate any nonsense off the miners, and if anybody stepped out of line they were to be dismissed. I was not willing to take that stance as I believed in what the miners fought for, as I come from a mining family so I was told that I could apply for redundancy, which I did. I took my redundancy from the coal board and I also was able to take my pension out because of my age and the time I was with the coal board. I was also offered a job as a manager in a private mine which I am still doing, and to top it all I was asked if I would take a part time job as an inspector for the union, so no I did not get the sack, but if I had not taken redundancy I don't know what the outcome would have been, but I am happy I went."

Some of the men were saddened when the pit was shut, but some were not so sad. There was one man who was always saying, "When they shut this place I will burn my working clothes, and run around this place naked," which was just what he did surrounded by a crowd of laughing men he put his working clothes in a pile on the floor and then doused them in petrol, from a small container that he had bought and then set them alight and did a lap of honour around the colliery yard naked except for his safely helmet.

Chapter 23 (The ending)

Over the next few years the mines were being closed around the country, but it was not only the mines that suffered. There was a knock-on effect as industries that were linked with the mines such as the steel works, railways, and in some cases electricity all felt the loss of the coal mines. In fact in some areas the unemployment was put as high as half the work force, causing families to leave the areas where they were born to seek work elsewhere, leaving empty houses and making once thriving villages looking like ghost towns. Also the friction between men who worked and men who scabbed continued for many years, passing from generation to generation and in many cases continuing today.

In the South Wales valleys the few who scabbed are still not forgiven and are not allowed into the working men's clubs. Nottingham and those areas where the scab culture was far worse than the valleys have also suffered causing splits in families and friendships that had long been united. There was a report that a man had been killed in a fight after an argument between members of opposing unions some years after the strike had ended showing the simmering amount of anger that this dispute had left on many people.

In 1994 the coal industry was privatised being renamed R.J.B. Mining, although it is now known as British Coal.
During the years leading up to privatising from the end of the strike there was a rapid closure of the mines in all areas, even the mines in Nottingham, which they thought would be safe, were savaged by the government that they had supported.

At the time when the mines were privatised in December of 1994 there were fifteen deep mines which belonged to the Coal Board, by March 2005 there were a total of eight deep mines remaining. This coupled with 174 working mines in 1983 before the strike and by 2009 there were six mines left.

During the strike the miners' leaders constantly told the media that the then National Coal Board had a long term plan to slaughter the coal industry in this country, and this was seemingly being put into practice as the miners seemed to have lost the will to fight, despite the fact that people seemed to have more sympathy for the miners now than at towards the end of the strike.

Many areas still today are feeling the effect of the strike, while others have seemed to recover and now have a good standard of living, but one thing that every mining area and village have in common be it a working area or a striking area the cuts and scars run deep and there will always be a story to be told and, although some may in time forgive the ones who returned to work nobody who saw this bitter struggle out to the end will ever forget.

A lot of the characters in this story are not with us now, but their mark on this journey will for ever be there.
We have lost Lou, Leighton, King Will, (who those who know him say he is now a union leader in heaven) DD, and Big Jones who was the inspiration behind this story.He was a great big bear like man, who as King Will once put it, "The mines are a tough and uncompromising place, and if you are to survive you have to be as tough and uncompromising as it is otherwise it will swallow you up."

Big Jones was not only tough and uncompromising but he was also as hard as the coal that he mined, (or as he called it black diamond), but he also had a sensitive side. One instance was when he saw a kitten being chased by two dogs under a parked car opposite the colliery. Being a man who had always had dogs he had no fear of them, so he just marched over and chased them away. He then got the kitten out from under the car, picking it up in his massive bear like hands. He then proceeded to knock on all the doors in the street until he found the owners of the kitten, where he handed it over safely and walked away not giving it a second thought.

You were taken from us in an untimely end
My inspiration, my hero, my life long friend.
You arrived above with a smile on your face
Making heaven a much brighter place.
When you got to those pearly gates
You were met there by all of your mates:
King Will, DD, and in front stood Lou
Who said, "Hello comrade we've been waiting for you."

Dedicated to
Big Jones (Much loved. Sadly missed)

(Loved you mate)

This is a true story of the 1984 British coal miners strike. It is a tribute to a group of friends and work mates who stayed out for the duration of the strike.
The stories are all true, but some of the names have been changed, but they all know who they are, although a few of them have now sadly departed this earth.

Wherever they are the bond between them will forever be there.
Cheers boys.

Thanks to all the boys in this story, you know who you are.

To all those who are no longer here, you are much loved missed by us all. Especially Big Jones, the inspiration behind this book. Wish you could have been here for it, you would have had a few words of wisdom for me.

To Bev Trounce for finding the cover photographs.
And to Leslie Phillips, who took the photographs, and was kind enough to let me use them.

Thank you all.

Printed in Great Britain
by Amazon

54761189R00069